MAD ABOUT MAX

Holly Fuhrmann

ImaJinn
Books

MAD ABOUT MAX

Published by ImaJinn Books, a division of ImaJinn

First Printing February, 2000

ISBN: 1-893896-05-6

Cover design by Patricia Lazarus

ImaJinn Books, a division of ImaJinn
P.O. Box 162, Hickory Corners, MI 49060-0162
Toll Free: 1-877-625-3592
http://www.imajinnbooks.com

DEDICATION

This book is dedicated to two women who have brought magic into my life. To my mother, Patricia Erdely, who first showed me the magic that books contain, and to Dorothy Fuhrmann, who, through her son, gave me my very own happily-ever-after.

Note from ImaJinn Books

Dear Readers,

Thank you for buying this book. The author has worked hard to bring you a captivating tale of love and adventure.

In the months ahead, watch for our fast-paced, action-packed stories involving ghosts, psychics and psychic phenomena, witches, vampires, werewolves, angels, reincarnation, futuristic in space or on other planets, futuristic on earth, time travel to the past, time travel to the present, and any other story line that will fall into the "New-Age" category.

The best way for us to give you the types of books you want to read is to hear from you. Let us know your favorite types of "New-Age" romance. You may write to us or any of our authors at: ImaJinn Books, P.O. Box 162, Hickory Corners, MI 49060-0162. You may also e-mail us at: readers@imajinnbooks.com

Be sure to visit our web site at: http://www.imajinnbooks.com

ONE

Grace MacGuire's Neon roared down Interstate 79. She was anxious to get home, though her trip to New York City had been a success. The publisher was pleased with the success of her last book, and her editor had offered a three book contract with a heavy promotional allowance.

Grace's heart was light and her foot was heavy as Garth crooned about Ireland on her CD player. She sang off key at the top of her lungs. The air conditioner was cranked on high, the sun was shining, and everything was right in her world.

"Gracey, maybe you should slow down just a little," a voice, rising above her caterwauling, said from the front passenger seat.

Grace's singing turned into one very brief, very loud scream. Someone speaking from the passenger seat wasn't odd in and of itself, but it was pretty strange when you were alone in the car.

Except maybe she wasn't.

As thoughts of kidnappers and hijackers danced through her head, she cast a frantic glance toward the passenger seat. There was no one there. A quick glance in the rearview mirror didn't reveal anyone either. Maybe they were on the floor.

Trying to still her racing heart, Grace pressed her foot to the brake and forced herself to move the car to the side of the road.

As the car stopped, she cautiously peered in the back and found a vacant floor. Maybe she had just imagined the voice?

She turned the radio down and all she could hear was the hiss of traffic. There was no other sound in the car. She let out a relieved sigh and waited for the adrenaline rushing through her system to subside. She'd imagined the voice. Or, maybe it was some glitch on her CD? Whatever it was didn't matter. What did matter was that NO ONE was in her car.

There were a few drawbacks to writing fiction for a living. The pay was sporadic; some days the words flowed and some days they didn't; and occasionally a good line of dialogue woke her up at three a.m., and she just had to get up and write it down. But hearing voices while cruising the highway was more than just a little problem—it was the type of problem that required professional help. Grace was pretty sure they had medications to control it.

"You know," the voice started up again, "just because they raised the speed limit in Pennsylvania to sixty-five, doesn't mean you have to go that fast." The voice paused a pregnant moment then added, "Or even faster."

Those words are just like my mother's! Only the voice was different. It almost sounded familiar. Grace knew she'd remember hearing a sing-songy voice like that, and she couldn't recall ever having heard it.

"Yes, you do," the voice continued. "Remember that long talk we had when Augustus and Nettie were having all those problems?"

Grace clapped her hands over her ears and started humming an off-key rendition of the "Star-Spangled Banner."

"She doesn't want to believe we're here," the voice said.

"*We*?" Grace squeaked. She didn't want to talk to her imaginary companion, but seemed unable to stop herself. Another sign of her mental decline.

"Of course *we*," a different voice said from directly behind the driver's seat.

"You know the three of us always travel together. Safety in numbers and all that," came a third voice from the general direction of the back seat passenger side.

She looked in the rearview mirror and stared at the vacant seats. "Oh, say can you see," she sang, hoping to drown out her delusions. Her good mood evaporated and was replaced with a pounding headache.

"Can't you see the poor child's frightened half out of her wits?" the first voice asked. "I told you two to be quiet until I explained things to her."

"I'd rather not have anything explained. I think I'd rather you all just disappeared. You know like *poof*, you're gone? This is just a small breakdown that I'll forget all about tomorrow. You can all go away now." For good measure Grace added, "Please?" It seemed prudent to be polite to imaginary beings.

"Oh, turn around and look at us, you silly girl. We're not going to hurt you," the first voice commanded. "You've written about moments like this—how many times now—six, seven?"

"Like what?" Grace asked, still staring out the front window.

"Oh, you know, dear," Voice Number Two gushed. "The moment that the heroine meets us."

"Let's see," the third voice said. "There was Nettie, Pauline, Susan, Alice—and then that Spring sister trilogy—April, May and June. There have been seven books so far." The third voice dropped to a stage whisper, "I liked those Spring sisters a lot."

"And the fact that there were three of them," said Voice Two.

"Just like there are three of us," interrupted Voice Three.

"Would you two stop your chatter? You're going to drive the poor girl insane." Voice Number One was in charge, Grace realized. Or at least she thought she was.

"I am insane," Grace murmured as she dropped her hands to her lap.

Insane. Such a harsh word. She'd read the term *sanity impaired* somewhere not too long ago. She liked that better. Even if she was crazy, she'd at least be politically correct.

But why now? Her life was just the way she wanted it. She could understand if she'd lost her marbles a few years ago, when she was just a struggling, unpublished writer. But now, things were all going her way. Her life was perfect.

"Not quite perfect, dear," said Voice Number One.

"Please go away?" she asked again.

The voice was soft and soothing. "Now Gracey, you're not crazy. And we're not figments of that ever fertile imagination of yours. If you'd just look at us, you'd know who we are and probably even guess why we're here."

Reluctantly, she turned towards the recently empty passenger seat. A short, red-haired woman wearing a bright red sweat suit materialized. It was almost impossible to look beyond the brilliant color to glimpse her face, but...but then Grace didn't need to see the face because she knew just who was sitting in that seat.

"Myrtle?" The vivid older woman nodded her head, smiling broadly, increasing the glare her scarlet suit created by at least a kilowatt. With quiet resignation, Grace turned around and smiled at her back seat passengers. Voice Number Two was wearing a green sweat suit and had deep chestnut colored hair. She was not nearly as brilliant as her sister. "Fern?" Grace knew she was right before the woman in question nodded.

The last woman, Voice Number Three, was wearing a neon yellow sweat suit that made her look like a banana. Her hair was yellow, too. Not blonde, but a vivid, brilliant yellow. It only added to the banana impression. "Blossom?" Grace sighed when the woman also nodded.

There it was—she was crazy. There was no other explanation for finding three fictional characters—characters that she'd created—sitting in her car.

This wasn't just hearing a spurt of dialogue in her mind. This wasn't just waking up at three o'clock in the morning because a character wouldn't let her sleep. This was three characters suddenly becoming flesh-and-blood and crawling into her car to keep her company.

This was crazy.

"No, it's not," three voices chimed in at once.

Grace looked at them all. "It isn't polite to eavesdrop on someone's private thoughts. If you can't help it, the least you could do is pretend you didn't hear anything and wait until I actually got the words out my mouth."

"Like we just did?" Myrtle asked.

When Grace created her fairies for her fairy godmother books, she'd given them certain powers. They could appear people-height, although they could only manage about four feet on a good day, or they could appear fairy-height, around two feet. Right now, they were people-height. And, they could read their godchildren's minds. She was already beginning to regret that particular power.

"Yes. Like you just did." What exactly did they want?

"Well, we're here..." Fern began, answering Grace's unasked question.

"Not until I ask!" Grace yelled. She regretted it at once when she saw Fern wilt. "I'm sorry I yelled." She took a deep cleansing breath. "It's just, I'm a little on edge here."

Fern looked up and smiled. "It's okay, honey. After all, it's not every day a woman has her wish come true."

"I didn't wish you. I invented you for my books, but I didn't wish you into my car." But they were in her car. "I'm crazy," she moaned.

Crazy. Sanity Impaired. Nuts, flaky, bonkers, one brick short of a load, a little left of center—okay, a lot left of center.

"Now, you have to stop all that negative thinking," Myrtle warned. "It's not going to do anyone any good. We're not here to force you to wear that horrible white coat you're envisioning."

"And why would anyone want to tie your hands with the sleeves like that?" Fern asked.

"They wouldn't want her to hurt herself," Blossom instructed her sister. "Sometimes you become violent when you're not quite right in the head. Though why they make everything white when you're crackers, I don't understand. You'd think they'd go for a nice soothing blue or something."

"Will you two stop it?" Myrtle yelled.

Grace's head pounded harder. She never realized losing her mind could be such hard work or so very, very confusing.

"Okay," she said wearily. "Why don't the three of you tell me why you're here, and then you can be on your way again."

"Honey, you know why we're here," Blossom assured her.

"There's only one reason your fairy godmothers would visit," Fern said right over top of her sister.

"Quiet!" Myrtle yelled. This time it worked because the two sisters sat back in the seat and sealed their mouths. "Now, the two magpies in the back are right; you know why we're here. We're here to grant your wish."

"But I didn't wish anything," Grace said. "Oh, wait a minute. I did wish that royalty check would come in, so I could pay off my charge card. Did you bring it?" she asked hopefully.

Myrtle's brows drew together with concern. "Now, you know that's not the way these things work. We're here to help you find Mr. Right."

"I didn't ask for a Mr. Right."

"Yes, you did. Every book you write is a plea for Mr. Right. That's why you write romance, because you long for a romance. But more than that, you long for an everlasting, until- death-do-us-part, for-better-or-worse kind of love. You believe it exists. Just like a part of you believes we exist, so—*voila*—we're here to help you. And believe me you need it."

"I don't need you."

"You do."

"You do."

"She does," Myrtle agreed with her sisters. "We've been worried about you for a long time." Two heads bobbed their agreement. "We waited for the right moment, and it's finally here. Your job is stable, at least as stable as any writer's job can be. You were just thinking your life is perfect, but we all know it's not. You're lonely, and that loneliness grows more each day. Our job is to make your life perfect, to see that you find Mr. Right and live happily ever after with him."

"Please don't," Grace pleaded. She'd written about these three ladies seven times, and she knew firsthand what a muck they'd make of things if they started meddling. In every one of her seven books the fairies goofed. And most of the time it was a very, very big goof.

"Ah, but it always ends up with a happily ever after, doesn't it?" Myrtle answered Grace's unvoiced complaint. "We just thought we'd come and introduce ourselves, right and proper, before things start hopping. Although we really didn't need the introduction, did we, dear? You know the three of us almost better than we know ourselves."

Myrtle reached across the front seat and patted Grace's arm. "Everything will be okay, just go with the flow." The fact that Myrtle had touched her bothered Grace. She couldn't recall reading about illusions that had a physical presence. But then, she hadn't done all that much reading about mental problems, either.

"Go with the flow?" Grace moaned, putting her head in her hands and leaning against the steering wheel.

She was crazy. They'd lock her up and then throw away the key. Actually, Leila would probably take the key and wear it around her neck, telling everyone she met about her certifiable stepsister. Or maybe Doris would beat Leila to it. Neither liked her, that's for sure. And neither would mourn her loss.

Things couldn't get any worse.

She yelped when there was a knock on the driver's window. She swung around. As soon as she saw the police officer she knew that things could get worse.

Reluctantly, she rolled the window down. "Yes, Officer?"

"Is there a problem here, Ma'am?"

He was a stereotypical cop—big, broad, and giving her one of those icy cop stares he'd probably learned in the academy.

Talk about worse. He ma'amed me. First she was seeing and hearing things, and now some beefy boy with a gun, barely out of adolescence, was calling her *Ma'am.* This would go down in the books as the worst day in her life.

What would he think of the trio sitting in her car? Even though they were people-sized, they certainly weren't normal-looking, not by any stretch of the imagination.

"Ma'am?"

Grace quickly glanced at the other seats. The fairies waved.

"He can't see us, remember?" Myrtle smiled encouragingly.

In addition to their ability to grow or shrink, or hear other's thoughts, Grace had written that no one but the fairy-godchild could see the trio. That was one gift she might live to appreciate.

Hoping it was true, Grace looked the officer straight in the eyes. "I just got smacked with a blinding headache. I thought if I put my head down for a few minutes I might feel better." That much was the truth. Grace's head throbbed.

The officer didn't look like he believed her. He scanned the seats as if she might be harboring some fugitive—or something worse. Fairies would definitely be worse than fugitives, but the officer didn't appear to see anything.

"Gracey, we told you he can't see us. Honey, all your worrying is only going to give you an ulcer." There was a tinge of exasperation in Myrtle's voice.

"Watch," Fern said. She leaned forward and waved a hand at the police officer who didn't even bat an eyelash.

"Do you need medical attention?" There was a flash of concern in his steely eyes.

"No, what I need is less stress. A lot less stress and an aspirin or two."

The flash disappeared, and the officer was once again all business. "Could I see your license, please?"

"Sure," Grace said, pulling the piece of plastic out of her wallet while trying to ignore the three godmothers. Maybe if she ignored them, they would all go away.

"Not gonna happen." Blossom laughed.

Eying the officer nervously, she handed him the license. "The picture's not very good, but you can see that it's me. Actually, if I look as bad as I'm feeling, I ought to look an awful lot like that picture. You see, the guy that took it was drunk. I swear I could smell the alcohol on his breath. Anyway, he said smile and I -"

"Ma'am," the officer—Officer Rodanski, his name-tag proclaimed—handed her back her license. "That will be all. I don't think this is the best place to stop, though. If you think you feel up to it, you better keep going until you get to the next exit."

"Yes, sir." She breathed a sigh of relief. She'd just passed her first test. She'd interacted with someone, and they hadn't noticed she was crazy, hadn't noticed the three hallucinations that were plaguing her. Oh, she'd babbled, but she hadn't done anything more terrible than that.

"See, we can behave," Blossom said cheerily.

"Let's give her some peace and quiet to get used to the idea of us," Myrtle said.

"You'd think after all the books she's written, she'd be used to us already." Fern sounded disgruntled.

"Girls." Myrtle's voice was sharp. There was a slight pop and then utter, blessed silence. Grace peeked into the backseat. Empty. Maybe she was over her mental breakdown?

She started the car and turned the radio on low, no longer in the mood for jamming to music. She pulled forward into the line of traffic and drove on auto-pilot, ignoring the miles upon miles of repaving that invariably popped up on I-79 every summer. With all that work, it should have been one of the smoothest interstate highways around. Instead, it was one of the worst.

Traveling to Pittsburgh from Erie was nothing new for Grace. A lot of the time she could get her flights cheaper from Pittsburgh's airport than from Erie's, and it was generally worth the two hour drive. She frequently found the construction annoying, but today it didn't even faze her.

Today she was crazy.

When looking at the world from left of center, the road work didn't seem all that annoying.

Crazy. Grace MacGuire, romance author with a brand new contract, is crazy.

She half expected one of the fairies to pop back into the car, but they didn't. With relief Grace finished her trip in quiet, but there was no peace about it. She was crazy, and she was scared. Not a very peaceful combination.

***

Grace arrived home safe but a little less than sound. A glance at her watch told her there was still time to contact someone today. Rather than unpack, she looked in the yellow pages under psychiatrists. She was going to nip this little foray into mental unsoundness in the bud.

Thoughts of Doris and Leila lurked in the back of her mind. If they found out she was nuts, they'd... Well, she wasn't sure what they would do, but Grace was sure she wouldn't like it. No. She'd better not make an appointment, at least not a patient sort of appointment. The psychiatrist might practice patient confidentiality, but Doris and Leila could wring a confession out of a priest.

Her characters had gotten her into this mess; they could get her out. She'd use them as an excuse to talk to a psychiatrist. While she was talking, she'd ask about a character who heard...the phone ring.

"Hello?" She was nervous about speaking to anyone and somehow betraying her newly altered mental state.

"Is this Miss Grace MacGuire?" came a strong, totally unfamiliar male voice.

"Yes."

"Well, Grace, today is your lucky day. You're on the air with WWOW, the radio station that *wows* you with hits from the Eighties, Nineties and today. We have drawn your name for today's grand prize."

"WWOW?" She never listened to anything but the local country station, and WWOW definitely wasn't it.

"Yes. We've drawn your name, and you're the lucky winner of a free makeover at Le Chic's. Le Chic, where all your dreams come true.

"They will be expecting you there tonight at eight. The salon will be closed, and their entire staff will be on hand to create a whole new you. The whole works. You will walk out the doors a brand new woman. And this prize comes to you through the generosity of Le Chic and WWOW, the station that *wows* you with all the hits from the Eighties, Nineties and today.

"We'll send a photographer over and take a couple pictures of the new you—and all this is compliments of WWOW, your favorite radio station."

"Um..."

"We'll see you there tonight at eight," the voice said, and then there was a dial tone.

"A makeover?" Grace asked herself. Because she lived alone, she frequently talked to herself. Maybe it was another sign of her deepening psychosis?

She hurriedly scanned the list of psychiatrists on the page in front of her.

"Now, sweetheart, you're not crazy. The three of us are as real as that table you're leaning on. And you are as sane as I am." Myrtle was standing in the center of the room, wearing a hot pink tent dress this time. It clashed with her hair.

Grace shook her head sadly. "No, you're not real, and I am definitely not sane. You are just some strange manifestation of my illness."

The other two godmothers popped in. Blossom wore a pair of jeans and a bright yellow poncho, and Fern wore a mint green bathing suit and a shower cap. "I just popped out of the pool," she explained, embarrassment tinting her face. The other two godmothers looked disgruntled. Fern shrugged, and a lime green robe appeared over her bathing suit.

"Now, what's all this nonsense about Grace being crazy?" Fern asked Myrtle.

"She still seems to think she needs psychiatric help," Myrtle said.

"She thinks we're figments of her imagination." Blossom humphed indignantly.

"Figments?" Fern asked.

Grace nodded miserably.

"Could a figment do this?" Fern walked over and thwacked Grace on top of the head.

"*Ow!*"

"There, that should prove to you we're not figments. You

might write about us, but people have written about Einstein, Abraham Lincoln and Lazarus Long, and they're not fictional," Myrtle said.

"Lazarus Long is fictional. He's a character out of Robert Heinlein's books," Grace said, massaging her head. Her figment packed a powerful wallop. "I loved reading about him when I was growing up."

Blossom laughed. "Good one. Next thing you know, you'll be telling us that Glinda the Good Witch is fictional, too."

"She is." Grace was crazy, but the fairies were crazier if they actually believed in Lazarus Long and Glinda. Suddenly, she wondered if figments really could be crazy?

The fairies all suddenly looked serious. "You don't believe in Glinda?"

"Nope. And before you ask, I don't believe in Santa Claus or the Easter Bunny, either. And I don't believe in the three of you." She tried to sound like she believed in not believing, hoping that saying it would make the three elderly fairies disappear.

"It didn't work, did it?" Myrtle chuckled.

"What?"

"We're still here. Now, you better get ready for your makeover. The traffic to the mall is horrendous at this time of night." Myrtle gently placed a hand on Grace's shoulder and propelled her out of the chair, away from the phone.

"You're not coming with me, are you?" Grace asked the fairies. They all shook their heads, their expressions innocent. "And you won't be popping in on me in public, will you?"

"We could if we had to," Myrtle said.

"No one can see us, but you. Remember?" Fern asked. "You know, dear. You gave us our powers. We can't be seen by anyone but our godchildren, no matter what. We can go anywhere with you, everywhere with you, and no one would be the wiser."

"Except me," Grace muttered. Though wiser wasn't the word she'd use to describe herself at the moment. "Please tell me you won't be coming with me tonight."

"But we won't," Blossom said. At Grace's skeptical look, she hastily added, "We promise."

"Unless it's an emergency," Myrtle qualified.

"Will you be here when I get back?" Grace was sure facing fairies before bedtime was unwise.

"We're never far away," Blossom told her in a reassuring tone.

Grace didn't find the thought very reassuring, however.

Fern handed Grace her bag and her jacket. "Now shoo," she said, propelling her to the door.

Grace left, feeling as if she was standing in the middle of a mine field. There was no right move. Wherever she stepped she'd be blown to smithereens.

Or maybe she was Alice, gone tumbling through the looking glass. The way the godmothers talked, she had better be careful with her sarcasm. She might be hurting some fictional character's feelings.

"You just might," Myrtle whispered. "The three of us know we're real, but some of the characters begin to doubt themselves after a time. You could send one of them off the deep end. Then they'd have to see a psychiatrist. Wouldn't you feel guilty?"

Grace tried to ignore the delusional whispering in her ear. The godmothers weren't real.

Grace was merely crazy.

***

Grace faced Le Chic with all the enthusiasm of a woman going for her annual pap test. She didn't want to be made over, but being made over was preferable to spending the evening with her fairy delusions.

She forced herself to take the last couple steps into the building. "I'm the WWOW winner," she told the receptionist.

"Pierre's been waiting for you." The girl led her back to a private room where a ponytailed man jumped to his feet. "Pierre, she's here."

Pierre, the stylist at Le Chic's, took one look at her and said, "*Oo, la la.*" He clucked his tongue in a manner that didn't bode well for Grace or her appearance. Then he turned his attention to her fingers, which brought about even more clucking.

Grace tried to ignore his shocked look. After all, she liked to be comfortable. She wore her normal clothes—a sloppy pair of blue jeans, a grey t-shirt topped with a green, grey and orange flannel shirt. She carried a book-bag over her shoulder that served as both purse and brief case—her everything bag. A pair of old tennis shoes finished her look.

"When was the last time you had your hair done?" asked Pierre in a very fake, very annoying, French accent.

"Nineteen eighty-six, I think." If she hadn't been worried about not looking crazy, she would have laughed out loud at his horrified expression. Grace had discovered somewhere in the mid-Eighties, that if she wore her hair long, she could just throw it in a pony tail and go. It worked well for her, especially when she was up to her hips in a story.

"Well, we'll start with a deep conditioning and then a cut." He picked up a few strands of her dishwater blonde hair. "A few highlights—hmm." He stepped back and looked her over from top to bottom. "Yes, you'll do. At least you will after a facial, new make-up, definitely a manicure, and most probably an even much more needed pedicure."

"Girls," he called. He was immediately flanked by a battalion of his feminine cohorts. "It's party time."

Two hours later, dressed in a new outfit compliments of WWOW, Grace endured the cameras' shutters snapping and flashing.

"Now, you look," Pierre commanded her. With a flourish, he moved the newly bobbed, highlighted, made up, manicured and pedicured Grace in front of the mirror.

Grace gaped at the woman she saw there. She was clad in a micro-mini skirt that would have exposed her unmentionables at the slightest bend, a white silk blouse, and heels that were easily four inches high.

She, Grace MacGuire, was gorgeous. A knock-out. The type of woman men whistled at and pinched. She was stunning, lovely, easy on the eye, flawless, enchanting—she was perfectly beautiful.

She burst into tears as she hysterically demanded, "What have you done to me?"

The fairies had to have done this, and that meant they had to be real. No makeover, no matter how good, changed a Plain Jane into a fairy princess. It took a fairy godmother's, in her case three godmothers', magic wands to accomplish such a miracle. Either they were real, or Grace was crazier than she'd thought.

"Miss," Pierre said, and that only made her cry harder. The godmothers had even managed to change her back from the police officer's "Ma'am" into a "Miss" again.

"I have to go," she told the staff of Le Chic's and the photographers from WWOW. She fled to her car and made the trip to her house in record time.

Grace shut and locked the door, ran to her room, removed the ultra-fashionable clothes and fell into bed. She'd wake up tomorrow, and this would all have been a bad dream. A very bad dream. A nightmare. She'd be normal again. No fairy godmothers, no beautiful clothes or lovely face. Just plain old Grace MacGuire, the highly underpaid romance author.

Exhausted from the traumas of the day, she fell asleep. Dreams of golden carriages and handsome princes ornamented her sleep.

TWO

Grace woke up and stretched. She loved mornings. They were always so full of potential. Mid-stretch images of the fairies flitted through her mind. She groaned and slammed the pillow on top of her head. Maybe it was all a dream? A nightmare?

Maybe what she remembered from the day before was simply a byproduct of her exhaustion from the New York trip. Having a vivid imagination, Grace had experienced more than her fair share of nightmares, but this one was the worst one ever.

With trepidation, she walked to the mirror. One look at her image, and she dissolved into tears.

It was only eight forty-five in the morning, and she had just crawled out of bed after crying for hours last night. Instead of puffy eyes and a sleep-lined face, she stared at a beautiful reflection in her mirror. She didn't even have bed head!

As she got herself under control, she decided she'd wager a sizable sum of money that she didn't even have morning breath. This just wasn't right. Normal people didn't wake up beautiful. Not even beautiful people woke up that way. Nope, only the crazy ones did.

She felt the hysterical urge to either cry again or giggle over the absurdity of her situation. She needed to see someone about this problem before it got any further out of hand.

Grace ran to the living room. The phone book was just where she'd left it last night, open to the *psychiatrist* yellow page. She scanned it furtively, praying her fairies weren't watching.

Not wanting to take any chances, and having no previous experience with losing her marbles, she dialed the first name in the book. Artemus Aaronson. Now there was a *sane* name a girl could trust.

She could almost see him—elderly Einsteinish man with a pipe and wire rimmed glasses. He'd help her. Of course he'd help her, that was his job. But she'd have to trick him into it, so Leila and Doris didn't find out. She'd arrange a consultation for a *character*, not for herself. Yes, a character who was having problems with fairy godmothers.

He'd probably say there was some little pill she could give her *character* that would make her get over these delusions. Then Grace would just have to find a way to get it for herself.

The receptionist told her there were no openings, but she could get Grace an appointment next Thursday at three-thirty. Grace couldn't wait that long. Goodness knows what sort of beings she'd be imagining by then.

"Ma'am, I'm a writer on a deadline. I'm having a terrible time with some characters. I really just need to consult with someone on how they might react. Please, I'll take any time you can squeeze me in, but I have to see the doctor today."

"Well..."

"You know, I always mention all the people who help me with my stories in the dedication, Ms...?"

"Betty. Betty Borowski."

"Betty. And, if you get me in to see the doctor, I would consider it the biggest sort of help."

"I guess I could squeeze you in at noon," the secretary said, excitement in her voice. "Dr. Aaronson is done for the day at noon. Could you talk over lunch?"

"That would be wonderful. Thank you, Betty." Grace hung up and sank weak-kneed into the chair. She was taking charge of her problem, and she would overcome it.

"You don't have to do this," Myrtle said from behind her.

"You're not crazy," Blossom assured her.

Fern suddenly popped into the room wearing a ski outfit.

"The Alps," she explained. "And, no, Dr. Aaronson won't be able to medicate us out of existence. We're as real as Bilbo Baggins."

At Grace's skeptical look, Fern cried, "Don't tell me—you don't believe in Middle Earth,either?"

Grace shook her head, and Fern mumbled something about not wanting to be in Grace's shoes come Christmas morning.

"Go take your shower," Myrtle directed. "If you're going to see the doctor, you might as well look your best."

"You mean it gets better than this?" Grace looked weakly at her still gorgeous reflection in the mirror.

"Oh, lots better." Blossom offered her a reassuring smile that only scared Grace more.

But it turned out, Blossom was right. When Grace finished showering, she did look better. Much better. Her hair, shortened to shoulder length, fell into pretty waves that framed her face. At the fairies' insistence, Grace applied her new make-up, compliments of WWOW. It went on as if she'd been wearing it for years. No blobs, no smears. The results were impressive. She was gorgeous.

Wrapped in her bathrobe, she walked into the bedroom and opened her closet, determined to wear what she pleased, no matter how beautiful she now was—no matter what a certain trio thought. She'd just bought a new flannel shirt of muted greens and rusts. She'd give in enough to wear that, instead of one of her older, more worn ones.

"Uh, uh, uh," Myrtle scolded as Grace threw open the closet door.

Grace's jaw dropped open. Her closet was empty. Empty except for last night's outfit and one other.

The new outfit consisted of a pair of soft, grey pants and a pale pink silk blouse. Grey pumps sat underneath the clothes—the only shoes in the closet. Grace turned and ran to her dresser, jerking open the top drawer. Inside was what the godmothers must have intended to be underwear. Grace lifted it and eyed it critically. She didn't see how it would work. The stuff last night was a lot skimpier than her usual cotton fare, but these? There wasn't enough silk on the pile to cover her big toe, much less her assets.

She turned to the trio and wailed, "What have you done with all my clothes?"

"Now, honey. It's hard to catch a good man when you wear the things you usually do." Blossom's brow wrinkled in disdain. "Not that there's anything wrong with them."

"Not a thing," Fern parroted.

"But you have to realize that there are right ways and wrong ways to go about these things." Myrtle folded her arms across her chest.

"I like those things. They're comfortable, and I'm comfortable in them." A new balloon of hysteria formed in Grace's chest. She was hallucinating about fairies who made her beautiful and stole her clothes. She was much sicker than she'd realized.

Fern got off the bed and walked over to Grace, patting her shoulder. "Now, now dear, don't get yourself into a dither. You can have your clothes back after—"

"—you catch your man," Blossom finished.

"After your appointment with the doctor, you can go to the mall and buy more appropriate man-hunting clothes," Myrtle said.

"After my appointment, I have to work on my book. They've decided to go with the new series sooner than I expected." Grace hated working under a deadline, but she'd signed a three book contract for the series, promising the first of the Tanner brothers series next week. She was just having a little trouble wrapping it up.

"The mall," the fairies said together just before they all blinked out of the room.

It was too early to leave for her doctor's appointment, but Grace dressed hurriedly anyway. She wasn't about to sit around her house waiting for the fairies to return. If she was in public, maybe they would leave her alone.

She walked out into the bright sunshine and smiled despite all her problems. The winters were long and cold in Erie, Pennsylvania. Living on the south side of the Great Lake that shared its name, Erie was well acquainted with the term *lake effect snow*. Cold arctic winds blew over the warm lake waters and dumped tremendous quantities of snow on the entire region. But Grace had always thought that all that snow somehow made the rest of the seasons more special.

Out in the sun with no fairies in sight, it was almost impossible to believe she was crazy. Maybe it was all a bad dream? Maybe she'd go into the house and find that all her clothes were in the closet, and she was back to being passably pretty? Maybe...

"Maybe you'd like us to come along?" Myrtle asked, though she didn't materialize.

Grace's momentary good humor plummeted. No getting around it. She *was* crazy. She left for the doctor's not caring that she'd be early. She didn't even care if the fairies followed. She would ask Dr. Aaronson about her characters and pray that he had some helpful advice.

***

"Miss MacGuire," the kindly looking, white-haired receptionist called. Grace was the last one in the waiting room. She'd seen three other patients go into and then leave the inner office. She'd sat staring out the window at Erie's bayfront, worrying about her questionable mental state. The godmothers had, thankfully, not come to visit.

"Yes?"

"After you called I realized I've read your books. The fairy godmother books, right?"

Grace nodded, and Betty continued with even more enthusiasm. "Oh, I love those three. They're so sweet, and despite their mishaps, they always manage to have things come out right in the end. Are they the characters you're having trouble with, or is it the people they're playing Cupid for?"

"A little of both," Grace admitted.

"Well, you just go right on in. Max will help you out."

"Thank you. I won't forget that dedication." Grace smiled at the older woman as she walked through the door into the inner office. A high-backed, leather chair was turned, facing a window that offered the same view of the bayfront that Grace had been enjoying. Warm, dark colors dominated the room. There were oak book cases and deep cranberry walls with accents of green. The room was masculine, yet comforting.

Grace cleared her throat. "Dr. Aaronson?"

The chair swung around and, at her first glimpse of Doctor Artemus Aaronson, Grace gave a little cry. Her knees went weak, her palms started sweating, and her heart rate skipped erratically. *"Oh, my."*

"Pardon?" said the very young, very handsome doctor.

Where was Einstein, with the wire-rimmed glasses and pipe?

As she continued to stare at the man, she realized the fairies had planned this whole thing. They wanted her to meet the hunky doctor, so that he'd fall in love with the very new, very improved, very insane Grace MacGuire.

She stood mute, trying to decide what to do.

The good doctor looked confused. "Miss MacGuire. Betty said you write romance books, and that you're coming in to consult me about some characters in your book."

"A writer. Just a consultation. Yes, that's right. I wanted to ask about some characters." She shook her head violently and backed up toward the door. "But, I'm afraid I can't consult with you. I like my life the way it was before they came yesterday. I like my books and I really, really, really like my blue jeans and flannel shirts. I do not like gorgeous doctors."

Grace took a deep, calming breath. "I'm sorry I wasted your time, Dr. Aaronson. I came here today to ask you some...some background information for an upcoming book. There are these very unruly characters, and I was at a loss as to how to deal with them. But, I just had one of those flashes of inspiration." *Keep talking*, she told herself. She had to convince him she wasn't nuts. If he thought she was, she might have to see him—often. And that would be a mistake. She would be falling right into the fairy godmothers' plans.

"Thank you for squeezing me in, but I won't be needing your

services after all." She raised her voice for the godmothers' benefit. "The plot these characters were going to use won't work. I see that now.

"Thank you," she told the doctor who stared at her with a befuddled expression. Then she turned and fled.

***

Artemus Maxmillion Aaronson sat in his leather chair, chin steepled between his hands, and stared after the beautiful woman who had fled his office. She—he glanced at the chart—Grace MacGuire was a writer, coming in for a consultation on a story?

But she couldn't consult with him because she'd changed her mind? The characters who were giving her problems were about to be rewritten, and she didn't need to talk to him. That was a shame.

Something about the woman intrigued him. Maybe she'd come back in and consult him some time in the future. Max hoped she would, and he wished she'd given him the chance to say as much.

Max tossed the file onto his desk, told Betty goodbye and walked from his office. His original plan for the afternoon was taking his sailboat out on the lake. TGIF and all that.

But suddenly the idea had lost its appeal. Max wanted to go shopping.

He got into his Explorer and headed to the mall. There wasn't anything strange about that, he decided. He needed to pick up a couple of new suits. Until this morning, he hadn't realized how shabby he was starting to look in his old ones. Maybe he'd buy a tux, too. He'd been thinking about owning his own for quite some time, but had never gone to the trouble of getting one. Yes, he'd definitely buy a tux. How could he have gone this long without one?

***

"How could you?" Grace asked the thin air as she drove nowhere in particular. "How could you let me go in there expecting some gray-haired old man with wire-rimmed glasses and a pipe? Now he thinks I'm crazy."

"You think you're crazy. So what does the doctor's opinion really matter?" Myrtle didn't materialize, but her voice came through loud and clear. The logic of her statement didn't comfort Grace.

"*Wrong*!" she yelled, forgetting her window was open, and she was sitting at a red light. The man in the Jeep sitting next to her gave her a curious look. The way she was going, the entire city would know she was nuts before the day was over, and The Steps—Doris and Leila—would move in for the kill.

"Wrong," she repeated, more quietly this time. "I don't think I'm crazy. I *know* I'm crazy. I've spent one too many nights alone. That's what it is. Or maybe someone put something in those brownies I bought last week at that bake sale. It could be just some residual effects."

"Nope," came a voice. Fern, Grace thought.

"Where are you guys, anyway," Grace muttered as she braked for another red light.

"Waiting for you at your house," Myrtle told her. "So you better head this way right now. We have to talk."

A true silence filled the car, and Grace knew they were gone, at least for the moment.

There was no way Grace was going home to have a showdown with the trio. She was going to go to the mall. Not that she was going to buy the *man-hunting* clothes the godmothers wanted her to buy. No way. She was going to buy some new jeans and flannel shirts. Maybe even some flannel boxer shorts to go under them instead of the scraps of lace the godmothers wanted her to wear.

And sweat pants, lots and lots of sweat pants. She'd cut some off to make shorts for when the weather got a little warmer. T-shirts and cut off sweats for her summer-wear. Flannel shirts and jeans for her spring-wear. That would show the fairies that they couldn't push Grace MacGuire around.

She hesitated. There was a flaw in her plan. She was trying to prove something to her delusions. Maybe that wasn't the way to handle this breakdown. Things were going from nuts to certified asylum material.

Grace decided her fairy godmothers were pushing her too far. Delusions or not, she wasn't going to take it sitting down. Determined, and pleased she was taking back control of her life, Grace drove to the mall.

***

Sitting in the living room of Grace's house, three elderly women smiled. Things were going according to their plans.

"She's coming along nicely," Fern stated.

"I don't know," Blossom piped in. "I have a bad feeling about this. Grace is right. Whenever we try to help, something goes wrong. Remember poor Susan and Cap? We wanted to give her a disease that would make that dim man come to his senses. Well, he did come to his senses, but the mono hit poor Susan so hard it was months before she was up to thinking about his proposal."

"Oh." Fern frowned at the memory of that particular pair. "And then he fell off the ladder when he tried to climb to her window and serenade her..."

"I thought it would be such a nice touch. Every girl should be serenaded at some point in her life." Blossom wrung her hands. She was tired of defending herself on this particular point.

"He fell down and broke a hip. He was in that body cast for six months."

"Girls." Myrtle looked at her two depressed sisters. "We've planned everything out perfectly this time. Nothing is going to go wrong with our Grace. Since she wrote the books, part of the misadventures were her fault—her and that strange sense of humor of hers. This time we're taking control, we're masterminding the story. So there's no way anything is going to go wrong."

Myrtle smiled after her little pep talk. Fern and Blossom tried to, but their upturned lips didn't ring quite true. They, more than anyone else, knew how confused these things could get, despite the most careful planning.

"Don't worry," Myrtle said again. They all turned their attention back to their perfectly sane goddaughter, who was in for a big surprise.

THREE

Grace pulled into the mall parking lot fully intending to head straight to Sears and buy her jeans. Problem was, she couldn't find a parking space in front of the department store's door. Actually, she couldn't find one anywhere near the store.

So she drove through the mall's labyrinth-like parking lot until she spotted a space, the only one she'd seen in fifteen minutes of circling the lots. It was on the far side of the mall, the exclusive section she never shopped in.

Grace entered through the Webster's door, still slightly annoyed at having to walk across the entire mall to get to her jeans.

She'd never been in Webster's before. It was too exclusive for her taste. The kind of clothes they carried hadn't suited her look, or lack thereof. Their apparel would be perfect for her new look, though—quiet and elegant. Not that she was interested. Even if she was interested, she wouldn't give the fairies the satisfaction. She was doing cotton, not silk.

As she stepped into the store proper, she was blinded by a flash of light. "Here she is," a loud voice blared over a microphone. "Webster's one millionth customer." A man appeared in front of the shining light. "Can you tell us your name, Miss?"

Grace stared at the man, unable to speak. What had the

fairies done this time? Realizing the man still waited for her
name, she cleared her throat and said, "Grace MacGuire."

"Well, Grace, you are our lucky one millionth customer. You
represent a million people who have walked through our doors, a
million people who have found Webster's to be the ideal place to
shop for quality women's fashions. We'd like to thank you, and
through you, all our other loyal customers, by offering you a brand
new wardrobe."

Grace could feel her lips start to quiver. Not only was she
was insane, she was lucky. *Extremely and unreasonably lucky.*
She wanted to run screaming from the store, but she didn't feel the
need to announce her sanity impairment to the world. Instead she
smiled bravely. "Thank you."

Two hours later Grace was clad in a beautiful tailored pant
suit, carrying an Italian handbag and sporting her newly made
looks. She left Webster's and walked hesitantly into the mall
proper. The Webster's manager had arranged to have the rest of
her new wardrobe delivered to her house. She'd been measured,
poked and prodded, had even had her colors analyzed.

Earth tones, they'd assured her. Muted greens, browns, rusts
and grays would compliment her medium skin tone and
highlighted hair.

As she left, Grace assured the manager that someone would
be at home to collect the packages. The magical trio wasn't about
to let her miss out on a pile of new, beautiful, *man-hunting*
clothes.

"What else do the three of you have up your sleeves?" she
whispered as she strode past the fountain. Having nowhere in
particular to go—shopping for jeans seemed rather anticlimactic
now—Grace sank onto a bench. She turned sideways on it and
stared at the water cascading in the fountain.

"Penny for your thoughts," came a decidedly male voice.

"Jeese Louise," she muttered softly. "Don't you guys ever
give up?" She turned around, no doubt in her mind who would be
sitting beside her on the bench. She was right, and she wanted to
groan.

Instead, she said, "Dr. Artemus Aaronson, I presume." She could have scripted this move by the fairies. Indeed she had scripted similar scenes in her books. "Whatever brings you to the mall on a gorgeous Friday afternoon? I would think you could find better ways of spending a May afternoon when you don't have to work."

"Call me Max. I hadn't really planned on coming to the mall. I was going sailing." His brow wrinkled, as if he was trying to figure out a particularly difficult problem. "But I needed to buy a new suit and a tux. Damned if I know why I needed that tux," he said, looking puzzled, "but it will be ready tomorrow. As for the suit, well, I suddenly realized today how shabby this one looks."

"Oh my God, it's already happened," Grace gasped, not hearing anything the man said after "tux." The devious godmothers were having the poor doctor buy one, so he'd be all ready for the wedding.

Grace raised her voice slightly. "Planning the wedding already?"

She knew it was silly, but she was irritated at them. If they were going to fix her up with her perfect man, the least they could do was have him rescue her from some villain or soothe her fevered brow during some illness. Remembering Susan and Cap's misadventures, she rectified the last thought. Absolutely *no* diseases.

Maybe the fairies were wrong. Maybe Max wasn't the man for her. Maybe he didn't like writers? Maybe he hated romance?

Grace turned to Max. "Tell me, do you like romance?"

The question struck Max as odd. But then, writers were notoriously eccentric. But considering she talked to fountains about weddings, Grace was taking eccentricity to a higher level. Max was beginning to suspect that Grace MacGuire had a few more problems than a troublesome manuscript. "Uh, I like romance I guess. I used to send my girlfriend, Terri, flowers for Valentine's Day."

Grace laughed then, a great big, relieved belly laugh. Again she spoke to the fountain. "Ha! He has a girlfriend!"

Max looked around and aside from the small crowd watching Grace talk to a fountain, there didn't appear to be anyone connected with her. "Uh, we broke up last year. Irreconcilable differences. I loved her and so did she—love herself, that is. Seems she was a one woman kind of gal and couldn't see beyond her mirror."

Despite not wanting to like this fairy prince, she felt a wave of compassion. "I'm sorry."

"It was for the best. I think when the right one comes along, you know it, and all the problems don't amount to much. Our problems amounted to way too many." He shrugged his shoulders. "I would really like a chance to talk to you about your book. I know you've changed your mind about the characters, but I might be able to help, anyway."

Grace studied the doctor. Maybe he could help, but only if she watched her step. She would just have to be careful—very, very careful. "Maybe you could."

"Do you want to come back to the office and see me next week?"

Grace thought about dealing with fairies on her own all weekend. "I think the sooner we talk, the better...for my story. Do you have time today, since you're not going sailing?"

He smiled. "Your place or mine?"

"Definitely yours." She followed him out of the mall, purposely lagging behind. "You three just stay out of his house," she whispered. "No listening in, either. Do you understand?"

"Yes, dear," Myrtle whispered in her head.

"Did you say something?" Max was staring at her with curiosity.

Grace shook her head. Max shrugged and continued toward the door. Grace gratefully followed him.

"Where are you parked?" he asked.

"Outside Webster's." And she was sure she knew who she had to thank for the mysterious lack of other parking spaces, not to mention the pile of *manhunting* clothes.

"So am I. Why don't you ride with me? We can come back

for your car later."

Gratefully, Grace accepted. She wasn't really sure she should be driving in her current mental state.

* * *

Max lived in a condo on the lakeshore. The location of his home didn't surprise Grace at all. She loved the water. She'd only been waiting for a bit more financial security before she moved onto the shore herself. Of course there was her inheritance that would be coming next year, but she didn't really want to touch that. She'd save it for her future children, a great big college fund. If she didn't have any kids, she'd donate it somewhere, someday.

The fairies were good—very good, she realized as she gazed at the lake.

"It's not fair to use the water and seagulls against me," she whispered miserably.

As far as Grace was concerned, there was no sight more beautiful than Lake Erie in May. Max lived in an exclusive new development that stood at the base of Presque Isle, a natural Peninsula that was a major tourist attraction for the city, though it was really just outside the city limits.

The water stretched forever, much like an ocean view. Lake Erie was the southernmost of the five Great Lakes. Long winters basked in its shadow. But it was easy to forget them in the late spring sunshine, with the seagulls delicately arcing through the sky. Maybe she'd forget this mental aberration as easily as the winter's snows were forgotten when spring stepped into the picture and promised the summer to come. Grace hoped so.

She settled on Max's deck, an iced tea in her hand, looking out at the waves and gulls.

"So, tell me about your problem," Max invited, breaking into her quiet musings.

"Well, it's the fairies," she began.

"Homosexuals?"

Grace shook her head. This was going wrong already. "No, I mean fairies, like Cinderella's fairy godmother. Only I don't just have one, I mean write one, I write about three."

"I see," was all he said, wearing what Grace figured to be a patented psychiatrist's smile. They probably offered a class on it in med school. Patronizing Smiles 101 or something. "You're writing a story about three fairy godmothers, and you need a psychiatrist's opinion on them?"

"In a manner of speaking. Let me start at the beginning," Grace said. "I'm a writer, and three years ago I started a series of books, a series that's been doing very well. I'm getting more and more name recognition these days."

Realizing she drifted, she took a deep breath and tried again. "As I said, three years ago, I started this series of romances. Three slightly inept fairy godmothers..."

"We resent that," Myrtle said in her head.

"If you eavesdrop you can't expect to hear good things," Grace whispered.

Max stared at her, his eyebrows lifted in puzzlement.

Grace took a long gulp of her tea, wishing it was something stronger. Not that she drank, but since she was crazy what could a few drinks hurt, right? But she knew booze would only be a temporary fix. She'd rather have some very good prescription drugs that would wipe her delusions away permanently.

She jumped back into her narrative. "So, these three fairy godmothers—Blossom, Fern and Myrtle—help women find their own true loves. Only it's generally more complex than that when they start off. They do seem to thrive on making falling in love harder. And they don't always do things in a normal way. Just when you think everything's going to fall apart, somehow they pull it together."

"And these are the characters you're having trouble with?" asked Max.

"Trouble? Yes, you could call it that. You see, they showed up in my...ah, in a character's car yesterday. She's a writer, like me. I think every good writer has had a character talk to them, but this was different. I've had characters sort of show up—though not in the flesh—and show me...ah...*her* where they need to be, and what they need to do. But this time they were in the flesh.

I'm not sure what I should do for this character." She paused, searching for the right words—they were generally easier for her to find when putting them on paper or the computer screen rather than in person.

"Are we talking about a character, or you?" He was studying her. Suddenly, she felt like some lab specimen. As he watched her, waiting for an answer, she told herself to get up and leave.

Instead she heard herself say, "I'm not talking about a character. I'm talking about me."

She glanced up at him, expecting to see him looking at her with an expression of horror, or something. Instead, he gave her an encouraging smile.

With a sigh, she continued, "The three fairies showed up in my car. Then this," she tousled her hair. "This is the first thing that happened after they showed up yesterday. I won a contest from some radio station I never listen to." She imitated the announcer last night, "*WWOW, the station that gives you the best of the Eighties, Nineties and today.* I listen to country. But this WWOW gave me a complete makeover. When the makeover people were done, I didn't just look better, I looked fantastic.

"You wouldn't believe it to look at me," she went on, "but I'm not beautiful. I'm passably pretty when I put my mind to it, but most days I don't bother. I like sweats and flannel shirts, t-shirts if it's too hot. I wear sneakers, no make-up, and ponytails." She raked her hands through her bobbed hair, which, with the way the fairies were running things, probably only made it look more tousled and beautiful. "I generally don't even shave my legs in the winter."

Max just watched her and waited, she assumed, for her to continue.

"That doesn't happen to ordinary folks, does it? I mean, one minute you're passably pretty on a good day, the next you're gorgeous. I mean, I woke up this morning gorgeous. No bed-head, no morning breath—that's just not normal."

"And so you called me about three fairy godmother characters who were no longer just talking in your head? They'd come to life?" Max prompted.

Grace avoided looking at him. She didn't want to see pity in his eyes for the crazy writer. She watched a particularly active seagull dive instead. "Yes."

"But you ran out of my office."

"I couldn't go through with it. I shouldn't be here now. Don't you see? You're the one the fairies want me to have. It's all a set-up. With a name like Artemus Aaronson, you should be eighty, with gray hair, wire-rimmed glasses, and a whole passel of very well-adjusted grandchildren. Instead you're...you're perfect." The last sentence came out like an accusation, as if being perfect was Max's fault.

Max chuckled. "I don't know about the perfect, but I'm sorry I'm not a gray-haired grandfather. I intend to be someday, if that helps."

Grace shook her head sadly. "You couldn't help it. The fairies set you up, too." She sighed, already tired of fighting the trio. Maybe it would be easier to just give up and accept the inevitable.

"We might as well just get married now because they won't leave us alone until we do. They got you to the mall, even had you buy a tux..." She faced the water and yelled, "And just what is he going to need a tux for, eh, girls? Wouldn't be for a wedding or anything, would it?"

She turned back to Max and whispered, "Yes. You probably should marry me and get it over with. You can always divorce me quietly after you have me committed. I'd ask for my computer, so I can still write. But maybe that wouldn't be a good idea, considering my mental state. What if my next character is a mean, demonic sort? It wouldn't do to turn him loose on the city, now would it?"

"Grace, I don't think you're crazy. And I'm sure we shouldn't rush out and find a preacher. I'm a doctor. I can help you with this problem."

"I don't want to see you as a doctor." She couldn't take the chance of Leila and Doris finding out, and if the fairies were determined to make Dr. Artemus "Max" Aaronson her fairy prince charming, wasn't there a rule against doctors having a personal relationship with their patients? Not only would it be a conflict for him, but the way the fairies worked, he'd probably lose his license to practice psychiatry.

"I can recommend a friend to see you. I'll even set up an appointment."

"That might be for the best, but I don't think it's going to stop the fairies. They'll never let us walk away from each other."

He gently enfolded her hand in his. "Then we'll be friends."

"How do you feel about crazy friends?"

"Some of my best friends are crazy." He smiled. "And if you think my friends are bad, you should meet my family."

"Grace, dear, you're not crazy," Blossom said as she winked in and then out again right behind Max's chair.

"Oh, shut up and get out of here," Grace yelled.

Max gave her a startled look. "Now, Grace, how can I help you if—"

Frustrated, she cried, "Not you, them. They're not supposed to be eavesdropping." She scowled at the spot where Myrtle had stood. "Don't the three of you have anyone else to bother?"

"They're here?" Max asked, glancing behind him.

"Grace, you're no bother," Fern said, winking into view. "And, no, there's no one else. You know when we're working on a major case we generally take just one at a time. Oh, sometimes we make exceptions, if one case is exceptionally easy. Let me tell you, your case is not easy, and so we're dealing with just you." Fern winked out as quickly as she'd winked into view.

"I was right," Grace said to Max. "They won't leave until we're married. You might as well get it over with now. I'm glad you've decided to send me to a friend. I mean, I could never see you professionally, since we're about to become involved."

Max got up and started to open the sliding glass door. "Well, if we're going to get involved, I suggest we start with supper, where we can get to know each other a little better."

"Aren't you afraid of me? I mean, I'd be a little nervous if someone started shouting at fairies on my deck."

Max smiled. "It's not every day I entertain a fairy-phobic person in my home. But, I'm not afraid. You don't seem particularly dangerous."

It wouldn't be professional or scientific for Max to add that he had a feeling that Grace wasn't nuts, no matter how crazy she appeared.

He left Grace sitting on the deck and staring pensively at the seagulls as he walked into the kitchen. Max wasn't anything remotely related to a culinary expert. His bare pantry bore witness to that. So instead of cooking, he let his fingers do the walking and called for pizza.

He peeked from the kitchen at the woman sitting on his deck drinking an iced tea and watching the seagulls. To say he was in an unusual position was a vast understatement. Just what the hell he was going to do about it remained to be seen. But it would probably be interesting. Max peeked again—she was laughing at something, her face glowing like a beacon, making him want to draw closer. Yes, figuring out Grace MacGuire would prove very, very interesting.

The last piece of pizza was devoured. Grace realized she felt better. Oh, she was still nuts, but at least her stomach was full. "Max?"

He looked up, his expression telling her he was waiting to hear whatever she had to say. She decided Max Aaronson was an interesting man. He listened, really listened. That was a rare quality in a man, or a woman for that matter. He seemed to genuinely be concerned for Grace, despite her problems.

"Will your friend be able to cure me?"

He steepled his fingers under his chin, leaning his elbows on the table. "I'm not sure."

"That's not a very doctory thing to say. Shouldn't you be reassuring?"

He grinned. "Around you, I don't feel very *doctory*."

Grace told herself to ignore the comment, that she'd just be falling in a fairy trap. But she couldn't help asking, "How do you feel?"

"That's supposed to be my line." He laughed a moment, and then grew serious. "You intrigue me. From the moment you walked into my office you caught my attention. I want to understand you. As a writer, you've always heard characters in your head, but suddenly you're actually seeing them. Something is going on, and I don't think it's a psychosis. That's not a professional opinion, by the way, but a personal one."

He pushed back his chair, needing to put some distance between them. He needed time to figure out what was going on. "It's time for me to take you home so you can get some rest. I'll take you to the mall to pick up your car. We'll talk later."

"About?" She fidgeted with her glass.

"About Grace MacGuire. About fairy godmothers." He pulled out her chair for her.

Grace smiled as she rose from her chair. As they walked to the car, Max felt confused about Grace. He was like two separate entities. The doctor part wanted to maintain a professional distance so he could evaluate and possibly help her. The male part wanted to know this woman better. A woman who wrote of love. A woman who seemed so strong and yet fragile, all at once.

"I want to get to know you, Grace MacGuire. I want to understand about your work, about the fairies." He opened her door and then walked around to his.

"About the fairies. They claim that fictional characters—"

Myrtle cut in, though she didn't appear, "Only fictional characters that are well loved."

"Yeah, well, characters that are well loved are able to form a life of their own. It's as if their authors are parents and give birth..."

"Like you did for Myrtle, Fern and Blossom?" he asked.

"I guess." She squirmed at the thought of being the parent of the unruly trio. She might be crazy, but no one was nuts enough to want to claim that particular honor. So how was she going to handle her delusions? Better yet, how was she going to handle these strange feelings for Max? He fascinated her. The way he listened, the way he seemed to genuinely care about her, a virtual stranger. Gentle, yet strong. He made her feel safe and almost sane.

"We're going to figure this out, taking things one step at a time," he said. "After we pick up your car, I'll follow you home. We'll start by seeing if all your jeans and flannel shirts are gone. Maybe yesterday was just an aberration. Maybe everything will be back to normal. And I'll set up an appointment with my friend on Monday."

He kept saying *we*. Grace found the word comforting. We meant she wasn't in this alone. She had an ally. The thought held her fear for her sanity at bay.

"Grace, what happened right before you saw the fairies?"

"I was driving and listening to the radio on the way home from Pittsburgh."

"What were you doing in Pittsburgh?"

"I'd just flown home from New York. I signed a three book contract with my publisher." She'd been so happy. She'd thought she was on top of the world. If she knew then what she knew now, she'd have relished every blessedly sane moment of it.

"And are you worried about the books?" He glanced at her, waiting for her reply.

"Oh, no. I'm almost finished with the first one."

"So, you're excited about the books?"

She nodded. "I love what I do."

"How about a man? Have you had any problems with the men in your life lately?"

Grace felt as if she was playing twenty questions back in high school. "Are you going to ask about my childhood next?"

"Sorry. I'm grilling you."

"No, I'm sorry. You're trying to help. The only man who's been in my life lately is you. And you're not a problem."

He smiled. "I'm glad to hear it. But, what I'm trying to find out is what stress is there that might have caused you to—"

"Flip out?" Grace smiled wryly.

"That's not the term I would have used. But you get the idea. What new stress is there that might make your writer's imagination take flight?"

"Nothing new." She paused a moment. "You know, I can't decide which is the better option. Either I'm nuts, and the fairies don't exist—in which case I might never get rid of them—"

"Or?"

"Or, I'm nuts and they do exist. If so, they might never leave me alone. My only hope is doing what they want. Maybe then they'll leave." She fidgeted in her seat. "See? Hopeless."

"We'll work everything out, I swear. Why don't we start at your house and just go from there?"

"Okay." She sounded unconvinced.

They arrived back at the mall. Grace retrieved her car, and as she drove home, she glanced frequently in the rearview mirror, relieved to see Max was indeed behind her. Somehow everything seemed saner since she'd met him.

As they pulled up to the small Cape house, Grace felt her heart race. She didn't want to open the door. She didn't want to see the fairies. She wanted to run away from here and let Max convince her she wasn't crazy.

Instead, she got out of the car.

"Nice place." Max fell into step behind her.

"Thanks." She cracked the door. "Hello?" Silence was the only sound that greeted them.

Her home was the perfect size for a single woman. The furniture represented last summer's work. She'd spent every weekend shopping garage sales and putting her household in order.

She gazed fondly at the old cedar chest that sat proudly in front of her couch. She'd spent three weekends stripping, staining, and finally painstakingly painting it with four coats of polyurethane. She was proud that she'd done it herself. Just like she was proud of the small dried flower arrangement that sat on top of the chest. She'd grown them, dried them and then arranged them.

This was her home, something her furnished apartment had never been. Everything here bore her stamp. Though her stepmother and stepsister might sneer at the house's lack of size and its simplicity, she loved every inch of it.

She'd bought it—or at least bought what the bank didn't own—with money she'd earned through her own hard work. The success of her fairy godmother books allowed her more financial freedom. She'd inherit her father's money next year on her thirtieth birthday, but she didn't need it. She was content with making her own way in the world. Hopefully someday *her way* would lead to a place on the lake, like Max's. But until then, she was content.

Of course, if she was insane she might not be able to write. Then again, she might find that her work improved without the constraints sanity held on her. It was something to think about.

"Hello?" she called again. "They're not here," she whispered to Max when no one winked in or spoke. "Even if they were you wouldn't be able to see them. But then again maybe they are here, and just not letting me see them, either."

She called, "If you're here, come out. I want to talk to the three of you."

The house remained silent. "What's all this," Max asked, motioning in the direction of a huge mountain of boxes and bags.

"Oh, that. Webster's must have delivered the new clothes while I was gone. I didn't mention that, did I?"

Max shook his head.

"After I left your office, but before you found me at the mall, I won an entire new wardrobe from Webster's to go with the make-over. The fairies are efficient, at least sometimes. Alison, next door, has a key. I'm sure the godmothers saw to it she let the delivery people in."

He stared at her, questions in his eyes. "They're efficient?"

"Very. Except when they're making a mess of things, but even then, they do a killer job of it." Grace started for the bedroom. "Let's take a look at my closet. If there's still nothing in it that might prove something, though I'm not sure what. They stole all my jeans, so I'd be forced to dress up in these *man-*

hunting clothes. I guess they were afraid a professional man like you wouldn't look twice at a passably pretty woman who would rather wear jeans and flannel than cashmere and silk."

"I like jeans," Max muttered as they walked into her bedroom.

"And I like this room." Max eyed the quilt that Grace used for the headboard of her king-sized bed.

"So do I." She stared at her empty closet. Only the outfit from Le Chic's hung inside. "Yesterday morning this whole closet was filled to the brim with denim, flannel and sweatshirts. Now..." She shrugged.

"You know, the least the fairies could have done was hang up all that new stuff. Now, I'll probably have to press it all and I hate, utterly loathe, ironing."

Max studied the closet. The empty closet. "This doesn't make sense."

Grace nodded, glad he was finally getting the point. "That's what I'm saying. None of this makes sense."

"What night is your garbage night?"

Garbage? She'd lost her wardrobe and her mind, and he was asking about garbage? "What?"

"What night is garbage collection?"

"Wednesdays."

"And all this happened today, right?"

She nodded. "Right."

"So let's see if your flannels and jeans are in the garbage. If they're not, we'll be able to rule out the possibility you threw it all away without realizing it."

She led him to the back yard and opened the garbage can. A stench immediately filled the air, and she waved her hand in front of her face as she said, "See. It's just garbage, but no wardrobe. It didn't get picked up this week because I was in New York."

"So all your clothes disappeared while you were gone? Could it have been a robbery?"

"Someone would steal jeans and sweatshirts? I don't think so." There was nothing truly worth stealing in her house. A thief could certainly find better places to hit.

"Let's check anyway. Humor me."

Back in the house, Grace went through her jewelry box. "This is the most expensive thing I own," she said, holding her grandmother's string of pearls aloft. "They're certainly worth more than my clothes were. Plus the television, the VCR, even my computer—they're all still here."

"Cash?" There was a prickling at the back of Max's neck, as if someone was staring at him. He glanced over his shoulder. There was no one in the room. Still, he couldn't quite shake the feeling that they were being watched.

She placed the pearls back in the box. "In the bank."

"Okay, so no robbery."

"So what next, Sherlock?" She pursed her lips.

What next? Max stared at her lips. Kissing her came to mind. He'd like to—

He shut off the thought. She was attractive, but she was in trouble and didn't need any more stress. Plus, he wasn't the type of man who acted on a whim. He was the kind of man who spent months getting to know someone. He wasn't into instant lust. He wanted more substance to relationships than mere physical attraction.

So why was he standing here with Grace, almost ready to believe in her fairies? Because his tendency to want to save people in trouble had led him to psychiatry.

And even if he wasn't officially her psychiatrist, kissing her was certainly out of the question. That didn't keep him from fantasizing about how those lips would taste against his.

"I can't," he said in a strangled voice. Again, it felt as if he were being watched, almost as if his mother was sitting in the room and watching every move they made, knowing every lust-filled thought in his mind.

"You can't figure out what's going on, either?" Grace asked.

That was close enough to the truth. He let it stand. "Not yet, but I will. One way or another, I will figure it out." He needed to get out, to get some distance from Grace and her problem. He'd be able to think more clearly and decide why anyone would steal her clothes, why she thought she saw fairies—why she stirred feelings in him that he couldn't understand. "I think we should sleep on this."

Her face fell. "Listen, if you don't want to get involved, I understand. I can handle things on my own. You could just leave your friend's name and number. It might be better if you cleared out now and let me work things out with him. Lord knows what those three will do next."

"I'm not going anywhere but home, and I'll be back tomorrow, first thing. You'll be okay?" He was staring at a chair, as if he expected someone to materialize there at any second.

"Hey, I'm already nuts. What else can happen?"

FOUR

Grace snuggled under the covers, willing sleep to come her way. Maybe if she got a good night's sleep, things would look better tomorrow. Maybe she was just having a little emotional break-down, and she and Max would be able to fix it tomorrow. Maybe she'd seen the last of the three fairy godmothers.

The bed sank.

Maybe not.

"Hello dear," said Myrtle, when Grace opened her eyes. The three fairies were sitting next to Grace on the bed.

"You're making progress. After all, you've met your own Prince Charming, and it's only the first day. So many of our godchildren can't tell the toads from the prince for what seems forever," Fern assured her excitedly. The fairy was dressed in a green sari today. When she followed Grace's gaze, she explained. "I was visiting some friends."

"Now, as Fern was saying, you are making progress," said Blossom. "Finding your Prince, though, is just the first part of the story."

"About tomorrow," Myrtle interrupted.

"I think I can handle tomorrow on my own. Max will probably drive me to a very nice sanitarium where we'll meet his friend. My new doctor will see to it that they put me in a very comfortable wheelchair and straightjacket. Then they'll pump me full of all kinds of interesting drugs." Grace smiled bravely. "I'm going to think of it as a vacation."

"You'd better not let him do that," Fern warned.

"Oh, no. You can't do that. If you do, then Leila will get herself named your conservator, or maybe Doris will, and—"

Grace shuddered and held up her hand, not needing Myrtle to finish the sentence. "With everything else that's been going on, I forgot all about Leila." And that alone let Grace know how bad things were. Forgetting about her stepsister's spitefulness was a difficult trick indeed. She glanced at the clock. "What day is it?"

"I think we're sometime in the twenty-first century," Faith said helpfully. "The time you humans use always confuses me."

"It's 2000," Myrtle added, a bit more specific.

"Oh, my, oh..." Grace bolted out of bed. "I'll talk to you three tomorrow. I'll deal with all my delusions then. But right now I have to know...though I'm pretty sure. What am I going to do if...?" Grace slipped on a new robe and opened the door. "I'll see you tomorrow," she called out to the fairies as she fled the room.

One by one they smiled and winked out of Grace's bedroom.

Grace rushed through the living room and into the kitchen. She had to be positive that tomorrow was the day. Maybe she was wrong?

She groaned as the calendar confirmed her worst suspicions.

She picked up the card Max had left her and dialed his number. "Max?" she whispered when he picked up.

"Grace?" came his groggy reply.

"Max, are you awake?" There was no response. "Come on Max, I need you."

"What time is it? It feels like I just closed my eyes."

"It's twelve-thirty or something. Listen, are you awake?"

"I guess. What's the problem? Bad dreams?"

"Well, the fairies were just here, and maybe they count as bad dreams, but they didn't get me into any mischief this time. But then I thought of Leila. She's beyond bad. She's a nightmare, and that's the problem. I need your help Max, and I need it ba͞

"Slow down, honey. Now, tell me about this Leila. Is she another character from one of your books?"

"I've used her for the basis of all my wicked villains, but don't tell her that, or she'll sue for slander or something," Grace replied. "But she's real flesh-and-blood, and, worse yet, she's my stepsister. My very wicked, hates-my-guts, wishes-I-were-dead, stepsister."

Realizing what she'd just said, Grace moaned, "This sounds like a fairy tale, doesn't it? Did Hans Christian Andersen ever write one about a psycho-writer with living characters, and a wicked stepsister and stepmother? Kind of a Frankenstein, Cinderella thing. Or maybe Sleeping Beauty. All I know is I created the three fairies, and now I can't get rid of them. But, no matter how good a writer I become, I'd be hard-pressed to create a character like Leila."

"So, was your stepsister in the room just now, too?" Max sounded genuinely confused.

Grace sighed. "No. Leila isn't a figment of my imagination, like the fairy godmothers are. She's my late-father's second wife's—his widow's—daughter from her first marriage. Does that make sense? A stepsister. She's beautiful—really beautiful, not fairy magic beautiful. She's also married to a rich—eats from a silver spoon kind of rich—businessman. And she hates my guts." Grace sighed. "So does her mother— my stepmother—hate me, that is.

"They hated me when my father was alive and hated me worse when he died. You see, he left most of his money to me in a trust, which I can't touch until I'm thirty, except for school. He wanted me to make it on my own before I had to deal with his money. Doris, my stepmother, went through her money fast, and now both she and Leila resent me. Leila has her husband Leo's money, but it's not enough. They think they should have my money, and they hate me. I'd give them the money if I could, but I can't do it because of the trust."

"So now you think you're in a fairy tale with a wicked stepsister and stepmother?" Max still sounded confused.

Grace continued, hoping to explain. "Tomorrow—well,

actually today—is their party and they always invite me, so no one knows they hate me. And I always go, just to annoy them. But, don't you see, if they know I'm crazy they'll have me committed and take control of me, just so they can get their hands on Dad's money. They'd like nothing better."

"Okay, so just don't go to the party."

Grace twisted the phone cord. "I have to go, or they'll know something's wrong and will start snooping and find out where you've committed me. Then they'll take over and—" She stopped. "And you've got to help me."

"Help you do what?"

"Help me go to that party and not look crazy. You can pretend you're my date. We can even tell them we're getting married, since the fairies aren't going to leave us alone until we do. Then you'd be in charge of all my money when I turn thirty next year. Leila and Doris won't be able to touch my inheritance or me. When you divorce me, you can even keep all my inheritance. I never wanted the money anyway. I was just going to donate most of it.

"Well, maybe I'll need half the money," she amended. "I'd like to live in a small place on the beach. I love the beach. If my writing is driving me crazy, I won't be able to do that anymore, so I don't know how I'll support myself without some money from the trust."

"Let me see if I'm following you," Max said. "You're seeing your characters come to life, so you're convinced that you're crazy. These characters aren't going to leave until we marry, so we should get married. Then I can commit you to a psychiatric hospital until you're well. Marrying you will also protect you from your wicked stepmother and stepsister. I'll get an inconvenient wife until you're well, but then you'll divorce me and let me keep half of your father's sizeable fortune. Do I have that right?"

Grace was relieved he understood. "Right. You just forgot about the party part. You have come to it with me and make me look sane."

"That could be the hardest part of this whole drama," he

stated dryly. "I'm not sure I can make you look sane because I'm starting to doubt my own sanity."

"Oh, no. I'm the crazy one. You're just the white knight who'll ride to my rescue."

"How do you know I won't leave you in the hospital and spend all your money?"

"Because you're noble and generous."

"And how do you know that?"

"Because Myrtle, Blossom and Fern would never let me fall in love with a knave. Only prince charmings will do for their god-daughters. The three of them might confuse some things, but they always pick a good guy. Always."

"Thank you, dear." Myrtle's voice sounded a little watery in Grace's ear, though she didn't appear and neither did the other two.

"I'll be there in the morning, and we'll figure things out."

Grace released a breath she hadn't even realized she was holding. "And the party?"

"I'll probably regret this, but it looks like we're going to a party."

***

A booming sound woke Grace up with a start. Realizing someone was at the door, she crawled out of bed and automatically checked the bedroom mirror. Still beautiful. *Damn.*

She stumbled to the front door and jerked it open, snapping, "What?"

"Let me guess. You're not a morning person?" Max was dressed in jeans and a dark blue polo shirt, looking more chipper than any person, sane or crazy, should look before noon.

"Morning? Is that what you call this?" She glanced at her wrist, but she didn't have her watch on. "What time is it?"

"Time for breakfast." He walked through the living room toward the kitchen.

"You brought food?" Donuts. Maybe cream cheese danishes? If she had to be up before lunch, she wanted something that made it worth her while.

He shook his head.

"You're making it?"

He laughed. "I don't cook. That's why you got delivered pizza last night."

"You think you can chase me out of bed in the wee hours of the morning and that I'll be so pleased I'll make you breakfast?"

"A guy can hope." He glanced at his watch. "And it's not quite the *wee hours*, is it? I can wait while you get dressed. Heck, if you cook breakfast, I'll even make the coffee while you shower." He shot her a pathetic look. "All there was at my house was left over pizza. I hoped maybe you'd take pity on me."

Grace resisted the urge to smile. It wouldn't do to encourage him. "Can you make a decent cup of coffee?"

"The best."

She nodded and left him to find his way around the kitchen while she showered. There was a good point about her new look, she decided as she finger brushed her damp hair into place. She could do no wrong. She looked wonderful.

Since the fairies had shanghaied all her clothes, she wasn't sure what she'd find in the closet. Unpacking her new clothes had seemed too overwhelming last night. She hoped the godmothers had seen that at least one outfit was ready.

One pair of khaki slacks and a peach silk blouse hung neatly pressed, waiting for her. Casual dressy. As she slipped on the outfit, she had to admit dressing up didn't feel quite as foreign as it had yesterday.

"It doesn't smell horrible," she said as she helped herself to a cup of Max's brew.

"My coffee skills more than make up for my lack of cooking skills."

She took a sip. "Not bad."

"Glowing praise."

She set the mug on the counter and opened the refrigerator. Staring inside, she asked, "What do you want for breakfast?"

"What can you make?"

Grace picked up a carton of eggs. "French toast?"

"If you make it, I'll eat it."

"Why do I feel that would have been your response no matter what I said I'd make?"

"Because you were lucky enough to see the extent of my cooking abilities, or lack thereof, last night?"

She laughed as she started gathering ingredients. "So now that you've softened me up, what are we talking about? Fairies, parties, evil stepfamily?"

"The party's not until tonight. The fairies aren't here, are they?"

She shook her head.

"So, let's not talk about any of it. Let's pretend we're friends. I just stopped by and you forced me to stay for breakfast."

She raised an eyebrow. "Forced you?"

"Hey, what can I say? You like to feed me." Max took at long sip of his coffee. He looked at home sitting on a stool at her counter.

Looking at him made Grace nervous. That he looked as if he belonged in her kitchen, bothered her. She didn't want to come to depend on him. Her stories about the fairy godmothers might all end *happily ever after*, but this was real life. "After breakfast, then what?"

"Then we're going to do something I rarely recommend clients do."

"And that is?"

"We're going to go into denial and spend the morning on my boat." Grace was ready to object, but Max cut her off. "I'll get you home in plenty of time to get ready for the party."

"Why?"

"Because you need some quiet time, with no stress. Because I want to get to know you." He hesitated a moment. "Because I couldn't get you out of my head last night."

A morning on his boat, no talk of fairies, or her sanity impairment. It didn't sound so bad. She smiled at the man she'd thrust into the middle of her chaos. "I think I'd like that."

"So, let's get going, the morning's awastin'."

***

The lake was perfect. Max's sailboat was docked at the foot of State Street. It was small enough for just one person to handle, which was a good thing, since Grace didn't know the first thing about boating. She just knew that she loved the feel of being on the lake.

She sat watching the waves, the sky and the gulls as Max steered the little boat.

"So, is it working?" Max asked.

"Working?"

"Are you relaxed?"

Grace, rocking to the rhythm of the waves, drank in the scent of the lake and considered the question. She smiled at Max. "I believe I am."

"Good."

"I know I can't run from my problems, my fairies, forever, but for this morning running doesn't seem such a bad idea."

"I believe it's just what the doctor ordered."

She grinned. "I believe you're right. So talk to me. All you've done is listen to me. It's your turn. Tell me about Max Aaronson, the man, not the doctor."

"I'm the oldest of three children. Nick's a lawyer, Joy's a professional do-gooder, trying to save the world. I like the lake, I like to read, I..." The cadence of Max's voice, echoed the beat of the waves.

Grace sank into her seat and let herself just enjoy the moment. No thoughts of fairies, no thoughts of evil steps. Just the boat on the lake on a perfect spring morning, and Max.

And Max.

Yes, he certainly made the day perfect.

It was a dangerous thought, one that would only please the fairies. And it was ridiculous to think the man she'd met only yesterday was perfect. Of course he had some flaws, and the sooner she found out what they were, the better off she, and this growing infatuation, would be.

Grace shut off the negative thoughts and let Max's tales of his youthful hijinks soothe her again. Maybe he wasn't perfect, but at the moment, he was looking pretty darned close.

***

"I'll be back by four-thirty," Max called as he headed for his car.

"Four-thirty." Reluctantly the slightly sun-pinkened Grace shut the door. She'd had fun. For four blessed hours they'd sailed. Despite her occasional depressed thoughts, she felt revitalized. Max had been right; it was just what the doctor ordered.

She looked at the boxes littering her living room floor. Sighing, she dug in. It would probably have cost her an entire advance to buy all these clothes. Soft cottons and silks, sturdy wools and twills and lacy underthings that any Madam walking the street would envy, greeted Grace's eyes. There was everything—everything except flannel and denim. Reluctantly she admitted to herself it might be fun dressing in something different. At least for a while.

"We're glad you like them," Myrtle said.

She'd allowed herself to believe for a few blessed hours that the fairy godmothers had been just some momentary mental aberration. But, her denial hadn't lasted long enough. It had been too much to hope that they would leave her alone.

"I figured you'd show up."

"Of course we showed up," Fern admonished her. "It's part of the contract. We have to help you get ready for the ball." Excitement was apparent in all three expectant-looking faces.

"It's not a ball. It's just a party at my stepsister's place." Grace saw the disappointment in the godmothers' faces. A small niggling of guilt assaulted her. They might be imaginary, but apparently the three godmothers' feelings could be hurt. "But I'm sure it will be as grand as any ball. Leila wants the rest of world to see how the rich really live. I'm sure there will be caterers, and ice sculptures, and things like that. Heck, she'll probably even have caviar. You know, I've never figured out why, if you could afford not to, you'd want to eat fish eggs." Grace wrinkled her nose.

"When you turn thirty, you'll come into enough money to rival your sister's. Or, more accurately, your stepsister's husband's," Blossom reminded her.

"But I don't want it. Oh, I want enough so I don't have to worry about the bills, and enough to buy a place on Lake Erie's shore. Maybe enough to eat out frequently, because my cooking leaves a lot to be desired, though rumor has it Max's is worse. But that's it. I'll leave it where it is. Maybe some day, if I stop talking to imaginary beings, I'll have kids. They can have it."

"What do you have against money?" Myrtle asked.

"I just know there's more to life than money. Look what it bought Dad—a woman who loved him for his money. He eventually saw that money was all Doris wanted, and I think that's why he set my money up the way he did."

"What do you mean, dear?" Myrtle asked.

"Oh, I don't get the money until I'm thirty. You know, old enough to know I can make it on my own, and wise enough to be careful some guy's not out to marry me just for my money."

"And you're sure Max isn't?" Fern asked.

"Absolutely. He thinks I'm nuts, but he likes me anyway." She thought of the quiet companionship they'd shared on Erie's bay. "He's a doctor, so I don't think he's hurting for money."

"But I thought you said that most people didn't think there was ever enough money," Myrtle stated.

"Some people can't get enough money, but then it would appear that Max isn't some. He's...unique." She'd said it. Max Aaronson was unique.

He was good looking, but didn't seem to notice or capitalize on those looks. And he noticed things about her, other than her newly improved visual enhancement. He was... *Damn*, he was almost perfect.

"So, now that you've got these unpacked, let's get them all put away." Myrtle gave a slight wave of her hand, and the piles of clothes disappeared from the living room floor, along with the bags and boxes. Only one garment bag remained, hanging from the closet door.

"You could have done that last night." Grace felt a wave of relief. She really hadn't wanted to hang all those clothes up.

"No, that would be like opening your Christmas presents." Blossom frowned. "We would have taken all the fun out of your new clothes."

"In all this stuff did you manage to find a dress for tonight?"

"Yes. Oh, yes. Wait until you see it," came three breathless replies

"We spent most of last night working on it," Myrtle told her goddaughter as she led her to the garment bag.

Grace unzipped it, feeling a bit like a child at Christmas.

"Oh, my!" was the best response she could muster. The dress was perfect. Cinderella couldn't have been gowned any better.

"We argued for hours about the color," Myrtle said.

Fern was nodding so hard that Grace worried about whiplash. "We couldn't decide, so we finally called Glinda...oops."

"She doesn't believe in Glinda," Blossom said.

Myrtle broke in, "It doesn't matter if Grace believes in Glinda—Glinda believes in her. And she assured us that neither red, nor green, nor yellow were your colors." The three fairies were once again dressed in their particular colors. They were all wearing sundresses today. Fern's was a particularly ghastly shade of green—more puce than anything else.

"Oh, you don't like it?" Fern asked, once again reading Grace's mind, much to her annoyance. The dress changed from puce to lime green. "You're right, that's much better," the fairy said.

Grace broke her attention away from the fairies and stared at her own gown. Gossamer material hung from the satin-lined hanger within the bag. It was virginal white, but any other comparisons to a virgin stopped there. The material was almost indecently thin; Grace couldn't imagine what kind of underthings could be worn under such a dress.

"None," all three fairies assured her.

"It's not as thin as it looks. Nothing will show through. But you couldn't have the lines underthings would make," Myrtle explained.

"You're lucky you have the body to wear something like this," Fern told her happily.

"Yes. You perk where you should perk, and your bottom hasn't expanded, which is amazing considering all the time you spend sitting at the computer," Blossom added.

"I run." Grace groaned as she continued inspecting her dress. It had no sleeves. Actually, there was no top half at all. It would cover her breasts, but not by much. The clingyness of the dress would be all that held it up. "I don't think I can wear this," she told the trio.

"Oh, yes, you can," they chorused together.

She was still denying her ability to wear it a couple hours later as the elderly women stuffed her, rather inelegantly, into the dress. If she had written the scene, she might have described it as putting sausage into a casing. The fact that the dress's hem fell to the floor did little to lend it an air of respectability. Of course the slit up the side didn't help in that department, either.

"Max will drop his jaw," Myrtle buoyantly assured her.

"I rather like his jaw where it is." Grace lifted the gown's hem. "Did Webster's send any shoes over for this?"

"As we said, Webster's didn't do this one—we spent all night working on it," Blossom admitted.

"Except when you were eavesdropping on me," she accused.

"Checking in, not eavesdropping," Blossom protested.

"Shoes," Grace interrupted her. "I don't mean to sound ungrateful, but I don't think a pair of sneakers will cut it with this dress."

"Oh, no," Myrtle said. "You're absolutely right. It will take a special shoe to really show off this dress to its best advantage." And with great flourish she waved her finger, and a pair of shoes appeared on Grace's feet.

She looked down and was thankful to note they weren't glass. "Oh, no," Fern said. "Just think how impractical that would be. Why, if you broke one, you'd be spending the rest of the evening in the hospital having your foot stitched. Not very romantic at all."

No, the shoes weren't glass, just a deceptively simple pair of white pumps that sat on a heel so tall the laws of physics must have been tossing and turning over it. There was absolutely no explanation as to how such a tiny spike-heel could support Grace's five-foot-five-and-half-inch frame. But they totally suited the gown. "Do you think Max will like it?" she couldn't help asking.

"You'll know in a minute, dear, because he's pulling in now," Myrtle told her.

"Is there anything I should know? Any curfews or rules? I mean, you won't be turning him into a frog, or siccing dragons on him, or anything will you?"

The three women tittered and shook their heads. Myrtle spoke for the trio. "No, you just go out and have a good time. Just not too good a time before the wedding, if you know what I mean."

"There's not going to be a wedding. I like him. I mean, what's not to like? But I don't think marrying him would be fair." Grace tried to sound sure of herself.

"We'll see," was Fern's cryptic remark as all three of them winked out of the living room whenthe doorbell rang.

"Perfect timing," Grace muttered as she went to the door. "You're early." She drank in the sight of him. He filled out his tux beautifully. It was all she could do not to reach out and grab him. He was carrying a large box in one hand; the other reached out and took her hand as he stared at her.

She pirouetted. "Good or bad?"

"Wow," he finally managed, coming in off the porch and into the living room. "Very, very good." He studied her. "You know, at moments like these, the idea of your having three fairy godmothers seems more than possible, it seems plausible." Max handed her a box. "Uh, these are for you."

Grace opened it and found a dozen white, long-stem roses. She inhaled deeply.

"They're beautiful," she murmured. "Thank you."

She walked into the kitchen to get a vase, and Max dogged

her heels, asking, "Are you ready for tonight?"

Grace gave a mirthless chuckle. "As ready as any person, sane or otherwise, can be when facing my Steps. I'll warn you, they can be a bit much. And I guarantee that Leila will want you, if only because you're with me. But seeing how good you look in that tux, I'm afraid she'd have wanted you regardless."

"I thought she was married."

"And you think that would stop Leila? Nope, poor Leo never controlled her—never stood a chance, dear man. He had the proper pedigree and the proper balance in his bank account. He's even passably attractive. But I'm afraid he was never much at controlling Leila. I don't know many men who could. The saddest part of the whole thing is, I truly think he loves her.

"And then there's Doris. My dad was a strong man, but even he couldn't handle her."

Grace felt a wave of pity. Poor Max, he'd been pulled into the middle of this mess. "You didn't deserve having a psycho-writer and her nasty family thrown on your doorstep." She stood on tip-toes and kissed Max's cheek. The gentle gesture shouldn't have inspired the fireworks she felt in the pit of her stomach. But it did. *Oh, did it.*

Max's hand rubbed the spot where she'd kissed him. "Maybe I don't, but I'm sure glad someone thought I did. I can't think of anywhere I'd rather be." He reached for Grace.

Myrtle blinked into view behind Max and in Grace's line of sight. "Tell him not to mess the dress."

Reluctantly Grace pulled away. "Myrtle says you're not to mess the dress," she repeated for his benefit.

"They're here?"

"Myrtle is." Addressing the space behind Max she asked, "Where are the other two?" Max turned and pointed, a question in his eyes. Grace nodded.

"Oh, Fern had a yoga class, and Blossom's been chasing Merlin for centuries. He finally asked her out, so they've gone to dinner. But don't worry, she'll be done in time to see you at the ball." Myrtle smiled. "I'm keeping an eye on you until then."

"You think I need you to babysit me?"

"In that dress?" Myrtle laughed. "I certainly do."

Realizing they were being rude to Max, she repeated what Myrtle had said to him, then said to Myrtle, "You could let him just have a little peek, then neither of us would think I'm nuts."

Myrtle shook her head sadly. "It just isn't done. Only the godchild can see the godparent or parents. Now, if we were Max's, he'd see us and you wouldn't, but... Well, there it is. I'm sorry you're still doubting our existence. We'll try to think of something so big that even Max will be forced to admit we exist. If we can make him believe, then you'd have no choice, right?"

Grace repeated Myrtle's words to Max and then shrugged her shoulders. "If he believes, I'll be forced to admit you three are not just some manifestation of a nervous breakdown. But it would have to be pretty big. Big enough so that we can't write it off to coincidence."

"Then big it will be," Myrtle said as she winked out.

"She's gone," Grace told Max.

He glanced at his watch, "And we'd better be too if we don't want to be too late. Plus if we stay here I'm bound to try to mess the dress, and then we'll both be in trouble."

"Go," came Myrtle's voice.

"Okay," Grace said to both of them. This was all getting to be too confusing. The day before yesterday she'd been a normal romance writer, at least as normal as she'd ever been. Just a couple days later, here she was with a stunning man with humor and compassion. Three fairies dogged her every step, and she was on her way to her wicked step mother's and stepsister's. It couldn't get any worse.

FIVE

"Grace, my dear." Leila rushed up to Grace and swept her into an embrace that sent shudders of revulsion up Grace's spine. She wished she hadn't sent Max to park the car. He would have provided a small buffer between her and her stepsister.

Leila was beautiful. Her hair was gypsy black, her features finely sculpted, her body tall and thin. But expressions that flitted across her face kept her from being truly beautiful; they were hard and cold.

"I'm so glad you could come. I know how you hate parties." Leila took a step back and stared at Grace. "What in the world have you done to yourself?"

Leila's beautiful face hardened as she inspected Grace from the top of her head to the tip of her toes. "Why, our little blue jean queen has graduated to adulthood. And to what do we owe this...astonishing change?"

"Let's just say my fairy godmothers' hands were in it." Grace was actually enjoying Leila's bemusement. Maybe the party wasn't going to be so bad after all.

Leila's brow furrowed, her dislike for this change in Grace evident. Her very elegantly clad toe tapped in annoyance as her eyes moved up and down Grace's body one more time. Her features distorted even more.

As Leila stood puzzling over Grace's sudden change, Max

walked through the door.

"And who are you?" Leila cooed, her annoyance forgotten as she extended her hand, a move Max pointedly ignored.

He watched her lick her lips like a cat who'd gotten into the cream and was hungry for more—much, much more.

He saw the woman undress him with her eyes and he blushed, something he hadn't done since Mrs. Tarmanski patted his butt when he'd delivered her prescription while working at a local pharmacy his sophomore year of college.

This was what Grace dealt with on a regular basis? No wonder she was seeing fairies. As he slid his hand possessively around her waist, his heart ached for her. "I'm Max Aaronson," he told Leila in his sternest doctor voice—the kind he saved for hysterical patients. It never failed to make them calm down. He hoped it would work its magic on Leila.

"My fiancé," Grace added. The look she shot Max begged him to go along with the charade.

"Ah, yes, Grace's fiancé." Max wasn't sure he wanted to play into Grace's delusion, but he'd promised to help her appear normal at this party. Exposing the fairies wouldn't be a help. Plus, the feline look in her stepsister's eyes made him nervous. Maybe thinking he was Grace's fiancé would keep Leila at bay.

"Fiancé?" Leila gasped. The announcement obviously didn't sit well. Leila scowled. "Your fiancé?" she asked Grace, disbelief in her voice. "Let me see the ring."

"Ring?" Grace asked stupidly, as Leila's question sank in. She felt a sudden tug on her left ring-finger.

"We haven't..." Max began.

Grace held up her finger, displaying it for both Leila and Max. A exquisite pearl ring glowed on her finger.

"A pearl?" Leila asked. That she was knowledgeable enough to see the apparent worth of the pink-hued ring on Grace's finger showed in the greedy gleam in her eye as she gazed it.

"Oh, definitely," Max said easily, acting as if he'd picked the ring out himself. "Grace could never wear diamonds. They're much too cold and hard a stone. But a pearl, a piece of the sea, is just the thing. Warm and living, just like she is." He squeezed her waist, and Grace relaxed in his arms.

"Well," Leila said, visibly trying to pull herself together. "Let's get out of the doorway and join the rest of my guests. The house is so big, and we've opened it all to our company, so everyone is spread out. But there's food and music and...well, make yourselves at home." With that Leila flew away, her eyes intently scanning the crowd.

"She's looking for Doris," Grace assured her newly acquired fiancé. "We can expect her to fly in on her broomstick at any moment."

"Where did the pearl come from? It's exactly what I would have chosen for you, *if* we were really getting married." He was willing to play along at the party. "So where did it come from?"

"The fairies. I'd never seen it; it was just suddenly there." Her voice changed, dropping slightly. "But it's not big enough to make you believe, is it, Max?" Grace began to see a small window of hope. Maybe, just maybe, the fairies were real. And if Max were to believe in them, the window would fly open, and she would wholeheartedly embrace the realness of the fairies. If he believed, then Grace could, too.

She wouldn't be crazy.

"Close, but no cigar. You could have had it before, and just slipped it on. I'm afraid you'll have to do better than that," he said, his voice a stage whisper, too.

"Grace," came a nasally voice behind Max. "What's this I hear about a fiancé?"

He turned, and there was an older version of Leila. They were both brunettes whose hair bordered black, though Leila's was darker. Both were tall, only a few inches shorter than Max's five feet, eleven inches. Lank and leggy, they both wore dresses that emphasized their figures to the hilt. Perfectly made up, perfectly coiffed. The only discernable difference between the two women was Doris's slightly older face. The mother's and daughter's dark looks might have been considered beautiful if they both hadn't been standing next to Grace. Next to her, they appeared over made up, over dressed and awkward.

"Grace?" Doris MacGuire repeated.

"Doris. This is Max."

Doris' eyes narrowed dangerously. "I'm Grace's mother."

"Stepmother," Grace corrected.

Doris glared at her. "Stepmother. But I practically raised her, treated her like my own daughter, though my lessons didn't seem to take as firmly with her as they did with Leila. So what's this about an engagement, Mister...?"

"Dr. Aaronson," Max supplied. "Max Aaronson. Ours has been what you might call a fairy romance."

Grace started coughing.

Doris shot her a warning look and returned to cross-examining Max. "What is your specialty, Dr. Aaronson, or may I call you Max?"

"Max is fine, and I'm a psychiatrist." He inched closer to Grace, his hand instinctively grasping hers like some sort of talisman.

Doris cast a speculative glance in Grace's direction. "Ah. A psychiatrist. Is that how you met our little Grace?"

Grace started to respond, but Max cut her off, "Sure is. Why she breezed into my office one day."

He didn't say anything about it being yesterday, but Grace couldn't believe he was going to tell her stepmother about her problem. He'd promised to protect her. She stamped her magical fairy heel onto his toe.

Max didn't even blink. "You see, she was having a problem with some characters and wanted some medical advice about what to do with them. Of course, I was more than willing to help. The attraction between us was almost...well, almost magical. Love at first sight, and all that. So I asked her to do me the honor of marrying me, and here we are."

"Yes, here we are," Grace echoed.

Doris' face was a barely disguised mask of anger. Grace was sure she had something up her sleeve. Doris had always loved setting up her victims, toying with them like a cat with a mouse's tail under its paw. "And speaking of here, Clarence is here, Grace. If we'd known about your fiancé, we never would have invited your old suitor, but," her lips turned upward in a cold mockery of a smile, "the damage is done and you'll just have to tell him to his face. He'll probably be heart-broken."

Doris aimed her next barb at Max. "The man was infatuated with our little Grace. But she didn't think he was good enough. She's always looked down at the men who run in the right circles. She considers the *right* circles a little too artsy for my taste. But maybe that's what happens when you have an...artistic nature. Your taste for the finer things withers and turns plebeian."

Doris patted Max's shoulder. "Until now, of course. Let me go get our poor Clarence, and you can tell him your wonderful news, dear." Doris was hustling away in search of Clarence.

"Phew, talk about playing the role of wicked stepmother to the hilt. And if I were really your fiancé, would I be worried about Clarence?" Max was surprised at how the thought of Grace caring for another man bothered him.

"Only if you haven't had your rabies shots. He's been a burr on my backside for years. Doris and Leila want to see me married to the proper sort. Someone who will force me to give up this *silly writing thing*." She sneered the last piece with the same annoying inflections both Leila and Doris used. "So they've been throwing us together at every opportunity. Wait until you meet him, he's—" She paused and, then whispering, added, "He's here."

"Grace, dear. My, aren't you looking exceptionally lovely tonight. Your mother told me you were here and asking to see me." A thousand years of breeding and pedigree might have existed just to create a man like Clarence. He wore a tuxedo like it was a second skin. His perfectly sculpted bone structure was capped by impeccably styled black hair. His smile was white and straight, but it didn't quite reach his eyes. Max doubted one woman in a million would notice the lack of warmth in those steel grey eyes.

"Yes, Grace did want to see you. She wanted to introduce you to me." Jealous. Max was jealous. Even with Grace's assurances that she had no interest in the snake, he couldn't stand Clarence. Couldn't stand the thought of him touching Grace.

"Yes," Grace said. "Clarence, you've been so close to the whole family, I wanted you to be one of the first to meet my fiancé, Max Aaronson." She turned to Max and winked. "Max, this is Clarence Darington the Fourth."

"Clarence." Max looked down at the man who was only an inch or so taller than Grace. "Nice to meet you," he boldly lied. Actually, Max could have gone his whole life without meeting Clarence.

"Fiancé?" Clarence asked Grace, choosing to ignore Max. "You've gone and gotten yourself engaged? What about us?"

"Us?"

"Yes, us. I've invested a lot of time in our relationship," Clarence continued, ignoring Max's darkening face. "I've wined and dined you—catered to your every whim and desire."

"The only wine we ever shared was here at Leila's. For Pete's sake, Clarence, we never even went out on a date. I certainly never had any whims or desires where you were concerned."

Clarence didn't even pause, so lost was he in his list of complaints. "I had plans for us. Next year, when you inherited your father's money, we were going to go on a world tour together. Then we would buy a cozy little mansion, settle down and have a few kids. But now you've gone and gotten yourself engaged to..." He jerked his head in Max's direction.

"You turn from a wallflower into a raving beauty, and then find someone else. Leila said you'd be lucky to get me. I just can't believe you would do something like this." Clarence turned and walked away, muttering to himself about women who changed their minds.

"That's what Leila intended for you to marry?" Max laughed, his jealously evaporating as the man retreated, and his good humor returning.

"Threw us together at every turn. He didn't want to invest too much time in me—he was waiting for the inheritance. Guess he planned to sweep me off my feet then."

"Instead, I swept you off your feet."

Grace shook her head sadly. "No, I swept you. Or rather, the fairies swept us both into my growing delusion."

She glanced around at the groups that were gathered, drinking and chatting, in Leila's huge living room. "Well, there's no hope for it. Let's mingle, and I'll introduce you to some family friends."

"Which part of the family? Yours or the Steps'?"

"We'll avoid the stepfriends and shoot for some of my father's friends. Much like me, Doris and Leila only invite them to functions where it is absolutely necessary. But they're the people I come to see. Leila's husband, Leo, lends her enough social position so that they all come. And Dad's friends have enough position that she can't afford not to invite them. It's a sort of Mexican standoff. But, I reap the benefit. These functions are only tolerable because of the friends who do come."

Max followed Grace as she circled the room, introducing him. He couldn't help noticing that Grace was glowing, her new look noticed and approved of by half a dozen older couples, quite a few of whom were her father's oldest friends. They all seemed genuinely fond of Grace.

"Oh, I've saved the best until last," Grace said as she pulled him back into Leila's giant living room. "There's Mrs. Martin and Captain Ellis."

An elderly lady with perfectly coiffed grey hair was talking to a gentleman dressed in the requisite tux. He stood with military precision by the large fireplace, where a cheery fired crackled behind an iron curtain, as he listened to the older lady.

"They're two of the dearest souls I've ever met. I think Mrs. Martin's been sweet on the Captain forever, and I think he's just as fond of her. But neither of them ever makes a move to act on it." She shook her head sadly. "So much wasted time."

"Maybe they're just friends," Max pointed out.

"Yes, they are friends. But I think they'd each like to be more than that. Something holds them apart, though. I can't figure it out."

Max chuckled. "Don't tell me I've gone and hooked myself

up to an incurable romantic? Never mind. Forget I just said that.
I should have guessed the moment I found out what you did for a
living. No one would write romances unless they believed in the
power of love. But I hope you're not planning to try to fix these
two up." They moved closer to the unsuspecting couple. "They
certainly look old enough to figure out what it is they want and go
after it."

"Sometimes people need a little shove." She rushed into the
older woman's arms. "Mrs. Martin."

"Why, Gracey, dear, what have you done to yourself?" the
older woman asked, approval in her voice. She pushed Grace
away, at arm's length, and examined her from head to toe.
"You've always been beautiful, but there is something different
now."

Grace grinned mischievously. "I can't take the credit. If I
look different it must be because I feel different. And I'd like to
introduce you to the cause of the whole thing. Max?"

Max stepped forward, and Grace continued, "Captain Ellis
and Mrs. Martin, I'd like you both to meet Max Aaronson, my
fiancé." She hated perpetuating the lie, but since she'd told Doris
and Leila, she was sure half the party had heard. Grace wouldn't
hurt the older couple's feelings by not telling them herself. Later,
she'd just tell everyone that things hadn't worked out. "Max,
these are two of my oldest and dearest friends."

The captain, who'd stayed in the background as the two
women greeted each other, came forward and took his turn at
hugging Grace. "Congratulations, sweetheart," the gray haired,
walrus-mustached gentleman whispered in her ear. Then Mrs.
Martin came back for seconds on the hugs. That done, the two
elderly people turned their attention to Max.

The captain extended his hand in wary greeting. "Mr.
Aaronson."

Sensing the challenge in the older gentleman's eye, and
recognizing it as a caring protectiveness for Grace, Max tried to
put his best foot forward. "Dr. Aaronson," he replied smoothly as
he shook the captain's hand. For as harshly as time stood on the

man's face, he still had a grip of iron. "I'm a psychiatrist."

"Oh," said two voices.

"Yes," Grace gushed, anxious for her friends to like Max. "He's been helping me with some stubborn characters that just won't behave. I mean, behave the way I want them to. They've been a pain in my butt, if you must know."

"We resent that," Myrtle whispered in her ear, but Grace ignored her, determined not to let her cloak of sanity slip in front of Mrs. Martin and the Captain.

"Yes," Max said, picking up the ball when he noticed a look of distraction flit across Grace's face. He was growing to know that look. One of the fairies was either present or talking to her.

He'd promised to keep her slightly impaired view of the world a secret, and Max always kept his promises. "Grace came into my office, and I knew right away that she was the woman for me."

He carried the conversation with Grace's friends as she inched closer to him, seeking protection in the circle of his arms. She leaned against Max, enjoying his strength while the four of them talked.

Suddenly, Grace saw Leila motioning to them. "I think the wicked step is calling," Grace said.

Max realized Mrs. Martin and the Captain must have heard similar remarks over the years, because they just chuckled.

"Well, you'd better go see what she wants," the Captain told them. "Otherwise, she might come over this way, and we'd have to suffer her company, too."

"Some friends you are," Grace teased.

"When you're in the military, you learn to choose your battles wisely. And I wisely choose to avoid the dragon lady if I possibly can." The captain's twinkling eyes belied his serious expression.

They all burst into laughter.

"We'd better go," Grace said to Max. "Because Captain Ellis is right. She's on her way over." She glanced back at their two companions. "Don't worry. We'll save the two of you, even if it means sacrificing ourselves."

Still laughing, Max and Grace made their way towards Leila.

"Where did you two disappear to?" Grace's stepsister whined. "I have some friends I'd like you to meet."

Grace's eyes met Max's, and she knew he was as thrilled as she was at the thought of meeting Leila's friends. "Of course." Grace decided it wasn't worth the trouble of evading the duty.

"Why don't you stay right here and let me track down Delilah and Carl. He's in investments and wanted to talk to you about that money you'll come into next year," Leila said slyly, eyeing Max for some reaction. "You did know our little Grace is an heiress, didn't you?"

"Grace told me all about the money, and the problems she's had with unscrupulous people currying her favor in hopes of getting a cut. But she doesn't have to worry about me. Doctors make good money, and it just so happens that I have a trust fund of my own. So, as you can see, she never has to doubt why I'm marrying her. We've been discussing setting up some charity with all her money. What was it you were thinking about, dear?"

"I was thinking about a grant for impoverished authors or maybe a dating service for single romance writers or the like," Grace teased.

Leila apparently didn't see the humor. Her brows knit together. "Really, you two should take this more seriously. Just let me go get..." and she melted into the crowd, calling back, "Stay right there."

Max hummed the theme from *Jaws*. "I have the feeling we're being circled while she waits for the appropriate moment to make her kill."

"I've had that feeling since the first time I met her. I could see the dollar signs in hers and her mother's eyes the moment they walked into the house. But my father was smitten, and there was nothing I could do to change his mind. He thought I needed a female's presence. I never could figure out why he picked Doris."

Grace could barely remember her own mother, but she did remember how much she'd wanted a mother to love her. When Doris first arrived Grace hadhoped her wish had come true. She was never   able   to   form   anything   more   than   a   congenial relationship with Doris, however.

Suddenly Fern's voice whispered in Grace's ear, "Are you having a good time, dear?"

"Yes," she answered softly. She turned to Max and in a low voice said, "They're here."

"Can you see them?" His eyes scanned the room as if he expected to spot them.

"No. But I heard Fern a moment ago. I have a very bad feeling. Do you think anyone so far has noticed I'm crazy?" she asked fearfully.

"They're all captivated."

"I... *Oh, my God.*"

"What?" Max whispered in her ear.

"On the mantle." She pointed. The fireplace in Leila's living room was huge. It covered the entire west wall. The mantle was just as big. Wide enough for an adult to sit on it and made of the same heavy white stone as the rest of the unit was made of. Definitely wide enough for two-foot-high, fairy-sized fairies.

"What about the mantle?" Max stared at the spot Grace had pointed out.

"It's them," she whispered. "They're on the mantle." The three fairies were standing on the mantle waving at her, grinning from ear to ear.

"What are they doing on the mantle?"

"*Oh, my God,*" Grace gasped again. "They were waving and now, well...now they're all dressed like saloon girls, and they're doing the can-can!"

Fern's foot flew up at that very moment and caught Mrs. Martin's hair, which didn't happen to be her own, and sent it flying. The wig soared forward and landed in the punch bowl. The usually jovial Mrs. Martin shrieked, grabbed at her rather bare looking head and rushed forward, desperate to retrieve her missing hair.

Unfortunately a large crowd was situated between her and her goal. Unheedingly, she rushed forward and, with the skill of a major league linebacker, the elderly lady plowed through the crowd. Captain Ellis trailed close on her heels, but despite his military background, couldn't quite make it through the amassing crowd.

"What the hell happened?" Max hissed in Grace's ear as they watched the melee.

"Fern kicked Mrs. Martin's wig off," Grace managed between horrified giggles, a problem that had haunted her since childhood. She giggled when other people cried. Maybe it was another sign of her madness.

She glanced back at the mantle where the three godmothers were still dancing to the music, seemingly oblivious of the pandemonium.

Max watched a waiter with a tray of champagne move closer to the fireplace, hoping to escape the riotous crowd. Max had seen Mrs. Martin's wig fly off, seemingly of its own volition, but what happened next was even stranger. The waiter, seemingly out of harm's way, suddenly dropped the tray and grabbed at his head. Almost as if he'd been hit.

Grace's horrified laughter evaporated as Blossom's foot connected with the waiter's head. "Stop it," she yelled at the fairies. "Can't you see you're making a mess of this?"

The entire assemblage stopped their running and their screaming and looked at Grace. She wanted to check and see if she was frothing at the mouth, but she didn't. Max gave her hand a squeeze and then led her toward Mrs. Martin, who was trying to retrieve her once grey, now pink, wig from the punch bowl.

Waiters appeared from nowhere and began cleaning away the spilled drinks. The three godmothers blinked out of their can-can skirts and into the appropriately colored evening gowns. All three, still fairy-sized, sat on the mantle looking contrite and sedate.

"I need to talk to you Grace," Clarence's voice said from behind her. Grace hadn't seen him. She'd been too busy watching Max as he helped Mrs. Martin retrieve her wig and then gallantly escorted her to the kitchen.

Grace sighed, unable to prevent the inevitable. She'd known that Leila and Clarence wouldn't be pleased. She suspected that

Clarence had promised Leila some kind of kick-back for setting the two of them up. "Yes, Clarence?" she asked, still half eyeing the godmothers who were sitting much too quietly for her peace of mind.

"I need to talk to you and thought we might find somewhere private to have our little conversation," he continued.

"Clarence, I don't really think we have anything to say. The only things between us were the few contrived meetings that Leila set up. We weren't lovers. We weren't even dating." Grace decided that Leila and Doris might view Clarence as a man with an impeccable pedigree, but Grace had decided long ago that Clarence was not the brightest bulb in the light socket.

"I was waiting—"

"Until I was closer to my thirtieth birthday to make your move. I know, but it doesn't appear—" Grace's words were cut off as Clarence's hand wrapped around her wrist in a vice-like grip.

"Clarence?" she asked, suddenly nervous.

"Outside, Grace," he gritted between clenched teeth. "I need to tell you a few things, and I'd rather do it in private."

His voice was soft and soothing, but Grace could sense something else in it—something that scared her.

"All right Clarence," she said.

She had no desire to cause another scene, but as Clarence dragged her out the back door, she looked pleadingly at the three godmothers. The trio shrugged, one after another, like some kind of wave at a professional ball game.

Clarence dragged her past the crowd milling on Leila's back patio and into the furthest reaches of Leila's perfectly manicured backyard. The farther they got from the crowd, the more nervous Grace became.

"Clarence?" she asked. "Could we talk here?"

"Just a little farther, sweetheart. It just so happens that I parked my van back here. It was so crowded out in front. But then it's always crowded when Leila throws a party. She's always been the popular one, the beautiful one." They reached the van,

and   Clarence opened the rear doors and roughly threw Grace
inside.

"Clarence!" she gasped, startled by his force.

"I've been meaning to ask you," he said, as he climbed in
beside her and picked up some nylon rope off the floor. "Just what
did you do to yourself? If you'd looked this good when we first
met last year, I'd have already married you, and we'd have waited
for your money together."

Grace started to squirm, but Clarence held her in place with
his knee and, using the rope, secured her hands behind her back.

When he'd finished trussing her, he pushed her onto a pile of
blankets. "Sit down and stay quiet. We wouldn't want you to get
hurt if we had an accident, would we?"

"Clarence, what are you doing?" Grace asked, terrified she
knew the answer. She struggled and kicked, but the dress the
godmothers had gowned her in didn't lend itself to easy mobility.
She'd have given just about anything for a good pair of jeans and
her flannel shirts right now.

"Clarence?"

"Ah, my love, I couldn't let you marry that doctor," he said,
a strange glint in his eyes. "Why, he would spend the rest of his
life with you analyzing every word you said, every book you
wrote. That wouldn't be all that pleasant, now would it? So I'm
saving you from yourself. We'll fly to Reno or Vegas and get
married there. Then you'll be safe."

He crawled out of the van and slammed the door.

Grace screamed, but there was no one around to hear her.
And even if there had been, she was sure the fairies would see to
it they didn't. The fairies. Her heart sank. Because of them she
was being kidnapped by a money-grubbing madman. Because of
the fairies she was being taken away from Max.

And suddenly Grace couldn't think of anything that could hurt
more.

The driver's door of the van opened, and Clarence climbed
into the seat.

"Let's go, Sweetheart. Vegas and our lifetime of married

bliss are waiting for us."

As the van moved forward, taking her away from Max, Grace knew that there were things worse than being plagued by fairy godmothers.

SIX

"Myrtle? Fern, Blossom? Where are you guys when I really need you?" Grace whispered, hoping Clarence wouldn't hear her.

"You called us?" Myrtle asked sweetly.

"Did I call you?" Grace hissed. "Did I *call* you?"

She gave way to a short burst of hysterical laughter. Her life used to be simple and uncluttered, quiet even. It was gone now. The quiet and the solitude had disappeared, much like her sanity. Gone, history, *finito*...

"Dear, is there a problem?" Fern asked. Then she added, "Blossom, move over, you're practically sitting on my lap."

"No, I'm not. You're practically on my lap. Myrtle make her stop."

"Girls," Myrtle admonished them both. "We're in a van and there's plenty of room. Fern, you sit on my right. Blossom, you're on my left." To Grace she said, "You seem to be upset."

"Upset? I seem upset to you?"

Clarence glanced over his shoulder into the back of the van. "Darling, I understand. My love for you is overwhelming, but you'll see. It will all work out. And we'll have such a lovely time together. I'm taking you away to save you."

"Oh, shut up." Grace had tried to be patient with her kidnapping, would-be husband, but he was trying her patience. Actually, she was pretty sure that Clarence would test the patience of a saint, something Grace wasn't. Saints weren't generally known for being nuts. But with their penchant for sackcloth and ashes, maybe someone should rethink that.

Clarence glanced back and eyed Grace suspiciously. "Your sister's right; you're nuts."

"That's what I've been saying," Grace muttered.

"Grace, what's wrong?" Fern asked.

"We've only done what you asked," Blossom added.

She kept her voice low, hoping Clarence wouldn't notice her conversation with the fairies over the radio. "Let's outline exactly what you've done to me, shall we?

"I was accosted on the freeway by three characters who informed me they were going to help me meet my own-true-love. A cop with pimples called me Ma'am. I won a make-over that did more than make me over. It reinvented me—even turned me from a ma'am back into a miss. I met the man of my dreams in a psychiatrist's office. I won a gorgeous new wardrobe. I fell in love. Three can-can dancers showed up at my stepsister's shin-dig and proceeded to wipe out half the guests and... Oh, yeah, I've been kidnapped by a would-be Romeo who wants to get his hands on all the lovely money that I inherit next year."

She paused and took a big breath.

"So, yes, I guess you could say I'm a little upset. The question we should ask now is, just what are you—my three, loving fairy godmothers—going to do about all this?"

"Grace," Myrtle said in her most reasonable voice. "You seem to have forgotten that you wished for this."

"*I wished for this*?" Every word she spoke moved up an octave on the scale. "When did I wish for this?"

"Didn't she say she'd like to get kidnapped, and have Max ride to the rescue—prove his love is real and all that?" Fern asked.

"Yes, she did." Blossom wagged a finger at Grace. "You know you did."

"I didn't ask to be kidnapped!" Grace protested even as it hit her just when she'd made this so called *wish*.

"Of course you did, dear. At the mall you thought that the

least we could have done was have Max rescue you from a kidnapping or a deadly illness. We thought kidnapping sounded more pleasant." Myrtle said.

"I said that the least you could do was let him rescue me from some villain! I didn't say anything about kidnapping," Grace told them. "As for this kidnapping being more pleasant, that's debatable. Clarence or a deadly illness. Gosh, I wonder which I prefer?" She raised her voice. "Clarence, do you think you're more pleasant than a deadly illness?"

He glanced over his shoulder into the back of the van. He shrugged and turned back to the road.

"Now, what are you going to do about this?" Grace whispered to the trio.

"Nothing," Myrtle said and then added, "Umph," as Fern's elbow collided with her ribs. "Would you two sit still."

"Nothing?"

"Nothing. Max will be along to rescue you," Blossom assured her.

"And how will Max find me? How will he even know who's got me, or, better yet, if anyone's got me? He thinks I'm crazy. Maybe he'll think I've just wandered off because I was delusional." Grace tried to figure out what Max would do. "I doubt he'll ever anticipate that I've been kidnapped by an ex-would-be-suitor wanna-be-husband."

"She has a point." Fern ended the sentence with a tiny moan.

"We didn't take that into consideration," Blossom added.

Myrtle hesitated a moment and said, "Maybe we should have had someone see Clarence carrying her off. But with the commotion inside..."

"The commotion that the three of you caused," Grace reminded them.

"I don't think anyone noticed a thing," Myrtle finished.

"So, I repeat, what are you going to do?" Grace wanted to scream with frustration, but more than that she wanted to wake up in her bed and find out these last two days have just been a bad dream—that she wasn't crazy, certifiable, sanity-impaired.

But then she'd never have met Max. And could she honestly go on without him? It seemed too soon for him to mean so much to her, but he did. She didn't know what to do about the kidnapping, or about Max. "So what are you going to do?" she asked again. "You could just untie me, and I'll jump out of the van."

"Sorry, dear. Another fairy rule, we can't rescue you." Blossom patted Grace's shoulder. "That's the hero's job."

"You wrote the rules, you know. So there's no one to blame but yourself for all these silly restrictions," Fern said.

"The hero doesn't know where I am, so how can he ride to the rescue?"

"There is that," Myrtle murmured.

"So now what?" Grace asked.

Three voices chorused, "I don't know."

Poor, mild-mannered Grace MacGuire—romance author and flake. She was not only crazy, but she was kidnapped with no hope—at least not if she was relying on the fairies—of being recused.

Every second was taking her farther and farther away from Max. Every second was taking her one step farther from her sanity. Grace suddenly found she'd miss Max much more than her sanity. Sanity was a highly overrated commodity, while no rating in the world could go high enough for her Max. *Her Max.* It had a nice sound. One way or another, she was going to find her way back into his arms.

"We have to have a plan," she told the trio.

"Like the plan we had for June and Darryl?" Fern asked excitedly. She had been the one to think of that particular "plan" after all.

Grace choked. "I was hoping we could come up with something better than that one," she said when the spasms stopped.

"Well, it turned out okay," Fern protested.

"Now Fern," Blossom jumped in. "You know that *the plan* wasn't without its flaws."

"Well..."

Blossom cut her comment off. "The baby on the doorstep was a nice touch, but when June got arrested for kidnapping—"

"She got off in the end."

"And had to spend three weeks in that jail cell with Rocky, that female pit bull—"

"She ended up having a heart of gold."

"And that strip search... Well, let's just say we need a better plan for our Grace," Blossom finished.

"Humph," Fern snorted, insulted that *her plan* was being ridiculed.

Grace was relieved the fairies didn't have a strip search planned for her. Poor June hadn't enjoyed it a bit. The character had had nightmares about it for the rest of the book.

"Now, girls," Myrtle placated. "Our Grace is right about one thing. We've made a muck of this particular plan. Almost as bad as poor June's incarceration." She was quiet a minute. "Whose idea was this?"

"Fern's," Blossom tattled. Fern was silent.

"Well, the four of us had better put our heads together and come up with something better this time," Myrtle.

***

Where was Grace? Max's gaze circled Leila's guests one more time. He hadn't caught sight of her since Mrs. Martin lost her wig.

"I just don't know what happened," the older lady said for the thousandth time. She had small bobby pins holding down what wisps of grey hair remained on her head.

"One minute I was quietly talking to Captain Ellis, and the next my hair was flying across the room. It felt like someone ripped it right off my head. But there was no one behind me, just the fireplace." She continued to cry. She'd been almost hysterical, but was finally calming down.

Max did his best to soothe the elderly lady, but his mind was on Grace—and the fairies that no one except Grace could see. According to Grace, the fairies were doing the can-can on the mantle right behind Mrs. Martin, and then her wig flew into the punch bowl.

Maybe Grace isn't crazy. Or maybe I'm going crazy.

He didn't know anything anymore. He just knew he was worried about Grace. Where was she?

"Excuse me, Mrs. Martin. I have to find my fiancé. I just realized that I need to ask her something."

The elderly lady smiled through her tears. "Ah, young love. You run along. Millicent is fetching me a handkerchief from her purse, and I'll just wrap that around my head until we get home." She kissed his cheek. "Thank you for being so kind to a silly old lady," she whispered.

"Ah, but I haven't seen a single silly old lady all evening," Max said. "I did, however, run into this young, stone fox who was really into pink hair. Never did smell any hair-spray that fine before, either. Smelled rather like champagne punch."

They both laughed.

"See you later, sweetheart," he called as he hurried from the room. "Leila, have you seen Grace?" Max asked, interrupting Grace's stepsister's frantic direction of her staff as they tried to clean up the pink mess from her white carpet.

"No," she shouted. She turned around and saw who was speaking and began to simper. "I mean, no I haven't seen Grace. Why don't the two of us go look for her?"

"Why don't I go look for her, and you go find your husband," Max countered. "It occurs to me that I haven't had the pleasure of meeting him yet. Since we're going to be related by marriage, we might as well get to know each other."

Leila brushed up against Max. "You can meet Leo later. Don't you think we should be looking for Grace?"

"I'll look for her myself. Thanks. You just take care of your mess." Max beat a hasty retreat.

Grace had been right about Leila. She was sending out signals that flashed like a lighthouse on a foggy night. She wanted him. But she was bound to be disappointed, because the only woman Max wanted was one slightly sanity-challenged author.

And he wanted her now.

Max searched the grounds, and then he searched every room in the house. The only thing he found was the missing Leo.

"Oh, excuse me," Max said as he poked his head into an occupied room. A man was sitting on the bed in his stocking feet and a tux, watching t.v. "Do you know Grace MacGuire, by any chance?"

The man jumped from the bed. "Sure. She's my sister-in-law. Why?"

"You must be Leo," Max said, extending his hand. "I'm Max Aaronson, Grace's fiancé. And I seem to have misplaced her."

The two men shook hands, and Max decided he liked the looks of Leila's husband. Leo was shorter and slightly rounder than Max, but he had a firm grip and honest eyes. Max always held that he could tell a lot by a man's eyes. Not necessarily the most scientific measure of a man, but it worked for him.

"Pleased to meet you. I didn't know Gracey was engaged. If I'd known she was bringing her fiancé to meet us, I'd have been downstairs." Leo's voice dropped. "I always try to hide when Leila and Doris throw these damn things. Crowds make me nervous," he admitted. "But Gracey's always been the nicest member of this family."

"I kind of like her," Max replied with a grin. "Now, if I could only find her."

"How about I put my shoes back on and lend a hand?" Leo asked, already retrieving his shoes from under the bed. "We'll track her down in no time."

No time turned out to be quite some time later. Leo and Max searched high and low, and still no Grace. At first no one else had been overly concerned, but the more time that passed, the more people who joined in the search. Two hours later, Max finally admitted defeat. "She's just not anywhere."

The car was still here.

"Leo, do you know Grace's phone number?"

Leo's eyebrow lifted, but he made no comment on the fact Max didn't know his fiancé's phone number.

"Hi, this is Grace and I can't come to the phone right now. I'm either out, or I'm swooning in my latest hunk's arms. Either way, I'm not answering, so tell me who you are and I'll get back to you."

"Grace, if you get this and went home for some reason call me at Leila's. I'm going crazy," Max told the machine, hoping she'd pick up, but she didn't. He hung up frustrated and a little afraid.

"Maybe it's time to call the police." Leo's expression was a grim line of concern.

"Yes. But I'm not sure they'll be able to do anything," Max said morosely. "Why don't you call them? I'm going to her house to see if she just went home. She's been having a bad time of it lately. Some characters in that new book are giving her trouble. Maybe she's got the machine turned down and can't hear me." He was grasping at straws and knew it.

Max hadn't lied to Leo. The godmothers were her characters, and they certainly were giving her problems. They were giving Max problems, too, for that matter. "I'll stop at my place on the way to Grace's, just in case she went there."

Max handed Leo a card. "Call me if you find something here. I've got my cell phone, and I'll carry it with me."

"Sure," Leo said. "And don't worry about Grace. You'll find her, and everything will be fine. We'll probably all laugh about this tomorrow night."

"Yeah," Max said, not really believing it.

Something was wrong. Very, very wrong.

***

"So, what's going on?" Grace hissed at the fairy godmothers. They'd gone to see what was happening back at Leila's and had just winked back into the van.

"Well, there appears to be a problem," Fern said tentatively.

"Problem?" Grace laughed then. She saw Clarence glance at her. He was giving her more and more questioning looks, not that she cared. She was crazy, she was falling in love, and she was kidnapped. Why would she care what her kidnapper thought?

"Of course there's a problem. There's always a problem when the three of you start meddling. Remember in the book with May?

You put her and Julian on a ship and shipwrecked them, thinking it would be romantic, and they'd see how much they loved each other."

"It was a good idea," Fern protested.

"It would have been if they hadn't ended up on different islands!" Grace had once seen humor in all her character's mishaps, but suddenly they weren't quite so funny.

"Now Grace," Blossom protested. "It turned out all right in the end. They found each other when everything was over, and that time apart convinced them they couldn't live apart any longer."

Fern interrupted. "And now they have a lovely little family. Two children last time we checked in. And May was expecting her third."

"Why, Julian even bought her that St. Bernard she wanted, even though he does complain about all MacKenzie's drooling," Blossom finished.

"Oh, that's so nice to hear. I've always wondered what happened to them after—"

Grace cut herself off, remembering they were discussing fictional characters. Actually, Grace was discussing two of her fictional characters with three of her other fictional characters. Going crazy was hard work. She practically needed a scoreboard to keep track of all her delusions.

"Are you telling me that you can guarantee things are going to work out for Max and me?" she asked the godmothers. "That I'm not going to end up married to Clarence—who only wants my money—and committed to some asylum? Can you guarantee that Max and I will live happily ever after?"

Grace was beginning to feel hysterical again. She was still tied up, cruising in the back of a van on her way to an airstrip. Then, if Clarence had his way, they'd have a quick marriage in Vegas, while the man she loved had no idea where she was, let alone that she needed rescuing.

"Just go tell Max where I am," she begged the fairies.

Myrtle just shook her head sadly. "You know that's not how

it works. You wrote the rules, remember? Even if we wanted him to, Max can't see us or hear us. Only you, our duly noted and certified goddaughter can see us, no matter what we want. I'm sorry, Grace." Myrtle actually sounded contrite. "I just don't know what else we can do."

"I'm sorry, too, and I don't have a clue as to what to do, either." Grace's spirit sank, and she stared at the sky through the van's side window. Every second took her farther and farther from the man she loved, and there was nothing she could do about it.

***

Max felt like he was going crazy. He paced through Grace's house. When he'd arrived, the door was locked. But instinct told him Grace would hide a key somewhere. He found it hidden in the garage, tucked under the mat in front of the door leading from the garage into the house. Real original, that was his Grace.

His Grace. It sounded like a regal title. Max liked the sound of it. He wished she was here with him, even with her fairy godmothers chaperoning. He wanted to hold her, to tell her he cared about her.

No, the feeling was more than caring, he admitted as he continued to pace. He felt as if Grace was a part of him. It had happened too quickly, but that didn't seem to make a difference. Having her disappear, knowing he couldn't talk to her or hold her, left a hole in the center of his being.

Yes, he more than cared for her. He loved her.

He explored the feeling a moment and savored it. *Dr. Artemus Maxmillion Aaronson loved Grace MacGuire!*

There was so much he didn't know about her. What was her favorite food? Did she wear braces when she was little, or was that perfect smile a gift from nature? She was a writer, but what authors did she enjoy reading?

He wandered about her living room. There was a small wooden box on a bookshelf. GKM. Her initials. He realized he didn't even know her middle name, and he wanted to. He wanted to know everything about her. From what kind of ice cream she liked to what season was her favorite. Everything.

He'd remedy that soon enough. Once he found her, he'd never let her go. He'd marry her, and maybe then those fictional godmothers would disappear. Grace could write about anything she liked in the future—anything but fairies, especially godmother ones. Of course, if the fairies remained, that would be okay. He wanted Grace, even if she was fairy phobic.

Books by Grace MacGuire lined the shelves. He picked up the first book and turned to the back cover. *Fairy tales can be delightful, until you find yourself in the middle of one. Nettie wakes up one morning to find three fairies are determined to find her a true-love of her own. The problem is, Nettie doesn't believe in fairies...or love.*

He concentrated on the words, trying to keep his mind off the author of those words. But his mind was on Grace. He reread the first page a second time and was saved from trying it a third time by the phone.

"Hello. Grace MacGuire's house."

"Max, it's Leo. Grace isn't here. The police say they can't do anything for twenty-four hours."

A lot could happen in twenty-four hours. In twenty-four hours Grace had affected him more than any other woman had in a lifetime. "She's not here, either."

"Something doesn't seem right, though," Leo whispered.

Max pounced on Leo's concern. "What doesn't seem right?"

"Well, Leila and Doris seem to be taking this all very calmly. Too calmly, if you ask me."

"So, ask them what's going on." Max genuinely liked Leo, but Leila was another story. It was evident she didn't like Grace any more than Grace—or Max, for that matter—liked her.

"I'm working on it," Leo said. "I just thought it might ease your mind a bit to know they aren't worried. I'll call if, no, *when*, I find out what's going on."

"You do that." Max feared that Leo wasn't going to be much help.

The characters in Grace's book, Nettie and Augustus,

captured Max's attention and kept him from worrying about the storm that was starting to brew. The three fairy godmothers held particular interest for him.

He thought about what he knew. Myrtle was the eldest. More level headed than her sisters, which wasn't saying much. She was fond of the color red and wore it exclusively.

Blossom was next in line. Her hair was yellow, not blond, and she dressed exclusively in that color. She followed Myrtle's lead and fought constantly with her youngest sister.

Fern. Brown hair and the least garish of the three. She dressed in greens and often set out on her own adventures. In this book, Fern tried hang-gliding, which she claimed wasn't as dangerous as her sisters seemed to think. They could all fly, after all. It was Fern who was responsible for the plan that went very awry in Nettie's and Auggie's story.

As worried as he was, Max couldn't help laughing at the three fairies' banter. He chuckled at the scrapes they led poor Nettie into, and it was all in the name of true love.

Nettie complained that Auggie thought she was nuts because he couldn't see her three guardians. The godmothers explained that only the godchild could see and hear them.

Maybe they'll make an exception this once, Max thought. And he was sure they could tell him...

He caught himself mid-thought. He was a man of science. How could he entertain the possibility of fairy godmothers? Last week he would have scoffed at the idea, but that was before he met Grace. Because of her, he would entertain any idea, no matter how crazy it seemed.

That gave him an idea, and he yelled, "Hey, Myrtle, Fern and Blossom. I seem to have misplaced Grace. If the three of you are real, then you know where she is. I'm worried. Not that I think she's crazy. I mean I'd be worried if she was a normal person. I mean, Grace is a normal person. Well, not exactly normal, or I wouldn't care for her.

"I don't just care for her," he continued out loud. "I love her." It felt so right to say the words. The only thing that would sound more right was saying them to Grace. It might be crazy to fall in love with someone so fast, but crazy or not, Max knew loving Grace was what he was born to do.

"Anyway, I'm worried about her. I think there's something very wrong here. She wouldn't just leave the party and disappear without telling me where she was going. Besides that, I drove. She didn't even have a car."

Max cracked his knuckles in frustration and peered around the room, waiting for the fairies to do something.

When nothing happened, he said, "I'm reading Grace's first book, and I noticed that sometimes when you three get involved things go... Well, they go a little differently than you expected. So if you've dropped her down a well or given her amnesia or something, hoping I'll rescue her, I can't do that without knowing how to find her. Just let me know where she is, and I'll do my best to be her knight-in-shining armor. Please, just give me some clue that will lead me to her."

Max felt foolish talking to thin air, but he'd do even crazier things to find Grace. He looked at his watch. It was five-thirty in the morning, the weather was growing even worse, and Grace had been missing for eight hours.

"Come back to me, Grace" he whispered.

It had taken him his entire adult life, to find a woman he loved. He didn't care if she was crazy or really did have fairy godmothers. He didn't care if she was beautiful or merely beauty enhanced, as she claimed. He knew she was beautiful on the inside. All he cared about was getting her back.

***

"How is Max?" Grace asked the fairies, when they popped back in after going to check on him.

She was still tied, and her arms were beginning to ache from their cramped position behind her back. Clarence had parked the van in the airstrip's lot, telling her they had to wait for the storm to blow over Erie before Clarence's friend could fly them out. Personally, Grace hoped the storm lasted long enough for the fairies to figure out a way to let Max know where she was.

"He's worried, poor man," Fern murmured.

"He read one of your—no, our—books." Blossom corrected herself."

Myrtle said, "He's even starting to talk to us, hoping we can tell him where you are. He thinks maybe we dumped you down a well, or gave you amnesia. He says he can't rescue you because he doesn't know where you are."

"He wants to be your white knight," Fern said.

"He doesn't care if you're crazy. He loves you and wants you back," piped in Blossom. The two younger godmothers pressed their hands to their hearts and swooned.

Max loves me?

SEVEN

Max loved her? Grace felt a spurt of utter joyfulness. She forced herself to ignore the feeling. Max loved her? No, it was probably just another one of the godmothers' ploys. They wanted her married off, and had proven they'd stop at nothing to accomplish their mission.

"We don't lie." Myrtle folded her hands over her ample chest.

"But maybe you stretch the truth a little?"

Fern's face was flushed. "Grace, I can't believe you said that, why—"

"Girls. That's enough. Grace doesn't know what she's saying. It's the stress of being kidnapped." Myrtle patted her shoulder.

"It's the stress of being nuts," Grace corrected.

"We're sorry," Fern whispered, on the verge of tears. "We're doing the best we can."

Grace wanted to yell that their best wasn't good enough, but she couldn't bring herself to hurt the godmothers' feelings, even if they were only figments of her imagination. She sighed. "I know you're doing your best, but isn't there some way you can tell Max where I am? Or at least tell him where Clarence is taking me?"

Myrtle shook her head. "We keep telling you that you're the only one who can see us and hear us."

"There has to be a way you can—" Grace stopped short as a

thought occurred to her. "Do you remember when the three of you were dancing on Leila's mantle?"

Three heads—one brown, one red and one canary yellow—bobbed up and down.

"And when you kicked, you knocked Mrs. Martin's wig off her head and into the punch bowl?"

"We didn't mean to."

"Leila's mantle was big enough to be a stage. We couldn't resist." Blossom smiled at the memory.

"I may be the oldest, but I enjoy dancing, too. And the one thing you can say for your stepsister, she only deals with the best. That band was fantastic."

"But the point is you were able to knock the wig off. Even if she couldn't see you or hear you, you were able to make contact with her." Grace was excited now.

"We've already told you we can't untie you. But maybe you want us to go knock Max upside the head." Blossom's grin showed just how much she liked the idea.

"No, but maybe you can write him a note. Tell him where I am, or tell him where I'm going. This storm can't last much longer, and then Clarence will take me to Vegas. I don't plan on saying the *I do's*, but I'm not sure what he has up his sleeve. I need Max in order to get out of this mess."

"A note." Myrtle snapped her fingers. "Yes, that will do nicely. And I'm pretty sure we won't be breaking any rules—maybe bending, but not breaking."

She rose from the the floor.

"Come on girls," Myrtle ordered.

The three fairy godmothers disappeared, and Grace was left alone with her thoughts.

***

The storm outside added to Max's anxiety. He stood at the window, wondering if Grace was outside. If she was wet, cold and scared. Maybe she was hurt.

The *maybes* gnawed at his gut, causing him more pain than if he'd been out in the storm himself.

He raked a hand through his hair. He'd paced all night, and he was exhausted. He decided to take a shower, sure that Grace—wherever she was—wouldn't mind. He needed to clear his head so he could keep alert.

When he climbed into the shower, he started with an icy blast of water. As his sleepiness receded, he turned on the hot water, hoping to relieve the tension in his muscles.

He stood beneath the pounding spray, running through a checklist of his responsibilities. He'd already called his office and left a message for his secretary to reschedule his appointments for next week. He hated to do it, but most of his patients were pretty stable. One week off wouldn't interrupt their therapy too much.

He'd also called Josh Stone, who'd agreed to serve as his back-up, just like he always filled in for Josh. They weren't partners, just good friends. Of course, when this thing with Grace was over he might end up as Josh's patient. He wasn't feeling all that stable himself and might need some therapy.

Getting out of the shower and feeling slightly refreshed, Max toweled himself and slipped on his pants. He wished he'd thought to bring clean clothes with him. The tux might be new, but he'd worn it long enough.

He scrounged through Grace's bathroom drawers, looking for a razor to scrape the stubble off his cheeks. If—no, when—he found her, he had plans for her, and bruising her fair skin with his beard stubble wasn't one of them.

***

"Girls?" Myrtle called as she materialized behind Max. He was shaving, oblivious to the fact that the bathroom now contained four people instead of one. "We have to hurry up and get Max on his way. The storm's dying down, and Clarence will be taking off with Grace any time now." Myrtle surveyed the bathroom, looking for a way to get the message across to Max.

"What time is the flight from Erie to Vegas?" Blossom asked.

Fern snapped her fingers. A book appeared in her hand. "Uh, oh. There's nothing that will leave in time. So I guess we'll have to schedule one." She snapped her fingers. "Now, there's a flight leaving the Erie Airport in forty-five minutes. It will take him to a connection in Pittsburgh. From there he'll have ten minutes to hop on another plane that will fly straight through to Vegas."

"Good work," Blossom told her sister.

"Thank you—I do try."

"Well, now that we have transportation for our knight, we just have to find a way to let him know where he can find Grace."

Myrtle again surveyed the bathroom, and she gave a very ungodmother-like whoop of joy when an idea hit her. "The mirror!" she screamed to her sisters.

Myrtle ran forward and, with her finger, wrote the word Vegas on the steamy mirror.

***

Max had found a razor and some shaving cream intended for a woman's legs. He decided if it worked on legs, it would work on faces. He started running hot water into the sink. The razor dropped into the water when the word Vegas appear in the steamy mirror.

"Vegas?" he said in confusion. Why in the world would he see Vegas written on the mirror? It didn't make sense.

He was going crazy, he decided. It wasn't Grace who'd lost her mind. He'd lost his. Grabbing the hand towel, he wiped off the mirror and tried to put the aberration out of his mind. It was just stress, he assured himself. As soon as he found Grace, he'd get back to normal

"He thinks he's crazy and just imagined our message," Blossom wailed.

"There seems to be a lot of that going on lately," Fern grumbled. "What is it about us that makes people think they're nuts?"

Myrtle raised her chin in determination. "Well, he won't think he imagined *this*."

Picking up the can of shaving cream, she shook it vigorously. Then she wrote on the floor, "Grace—kidnapped by Clarence Darington. Take to Vegas to marry. You catch plane in— "

Myrtle swore, a very unfairylike thing to do, which caused her sisters to gasp.

Flustered, an even more unfairylike action, she tossed the empty can in the bathtub and wailed, "*I've run out of shaving cream!*"

***

A strange noise drew Max's attention. He turned away from the sink and watched in disbelief as the can of shaving cream levitated inches above the floor. It looked like the can was writing something. Abruptly it stopped and landed with a clang in the bathtub.

Cautiously, he moved toward the writing.

***

"Here, finish with this." Blossom handed Myrtle an eye-lining pencil.

"Why didn't you hand me this in the first place?" It had been difficult writing in shaving cream. Blossom just shrugged and Myrtle glared at her and finished her message. "...orty minutes."

The three fairies smiled, satisfied when Max cried out, "Thank you," and hurriedly put his shirt and his tuxedo jacket back on. "I'll get her back," he promised.

"Let's go tell Grace," Myrtle told her sisters.

***

"Well?" Grace asked impatiently when the three fairies popped back into the van where she was being held. "Did you get a message to Max?"

Three faces nodded, their pleasure apparent in their beaming smiles.

"And he's on his way?" Grace asked hopefully. "He's coming to rescue me?"

"No, he's here," a voice announced from the door. Clarence, the demented would-be-husband, crawled back into the van.

Grace glared at him. "Go away."

"Why, Grace," he crooned. "You'd almost think you didn't like me, the way you carry on. But I know better." He patted her leg.

"I don't like you and this is a wasted trip, because there's no

way you can make me marry you." She tried to sound more
confident than she felt.

"That's telling him," Fern cheered.

"Oh, I don't think I'd be too sure of that." Something in
Clarence's voice caused a small quiver of fear to crawl up Grace's
spine.

He looked like a mean little boy gloating over a stolen toy. "I
have a great plan."

"And what kind of plan could that pea-sized brain of yours
come up with?" Grace taunted.

Clarence's face darkened. "I've always had a plan. I just
wasn't going to use it until you were closer to getting your
inheritance. But now, Grace, my darling, you've left me with no
other choice. You see, I have a friend, oh not the one who's going
to fly us to Vegas, a different one, and -"

Grace snorted. "You mean to tell me that a worm like you
has two friends? I shudder to think what manner of men they
are—and I do use the word men in its broadest sense."

"Enough," Clarence snapped. He shoved her from her sitting
position back against the pile of blankets, and she yelped as her
bound arms pulled.

She struggled to sit up, but Clarence sat next to her and pulled
her close. "I'm sorry, Grace. I shouldn't have shoved you, but,
darling, you've pushed me as far as I'm prepared to be pushed. I'll
give in to you on many things during our marriage, but I plan to
wear the pants in this relationship."

He sat on the edge of the blankets and pulled her close, his
arms circling her. Grace's skin crawled with revulsion.

"I can't believe you did this to me," she told the godmothers,
who lowered their heads in shame.

It was Clarence, however, who responded to her complaint.
"I'm sorry, darling. I wanted to give you more time, but your
engagement announcement at the party made me realize that I had
to do something now or lose you. I couldn't lose you!"

"Oh, please lose me," she muttered.

Clarence glared. "Now, as I was saying," he continued before

Grace could respond. "I have this friend who slipped me a little drug that will make you very compliant. He says it's safe, but I'd rather not experiment on you. So your choices are: go along with me, or I'll give you a nice little shot that will help you see things my way."

"Just agree with anything the weasel says," Blossom whispered.

Grace glared at the three godmothers, who stood at the end of the van, watching the revolting scene.

Fern cheerfully added, "Max is on his way, and we'll get him to you before this little rat makes you say 'I do'. Even if you do say the words, you can always divorce him."

"But he might get part of her money then," Myrtle said, her brow knit with worry.

"I don't care about the money," Grace reminded them.

Clarence's eyes glittered with avarice. "That's right, dear. You won't have to care about the money. I'll take care of it for you. Now are you going to cooperate, or should we give my friend's mixture a try?"

"Say yes," Myrtle said. "We'll fix this so that the rat doesn't get one red cent. Not that the money matters. It's the principle of the thing."

"I'll cooperate," Grace told Clarence through clenched teeth.

"A wise decision." He crawled toward the van's back door. "Mick, the pilot, said we'll be taking off in about five minutes."

As he slid out of the back of the van, Myrtle stuck out her foot. Unable to see it, Clarence tripped and went flying out the door and onto the pavement. All four women smiled.

"Are you okay, Clarence?" Grace asked with saccharine sweetness, barely able to contain her laughter.

"Yeah, I'm fine." He rubbed at a red spot on his forehead that Grace suspected would turn into a rapidly growing goose egg. "I'll be right back to get you."

He wobbled around the van.

"So, how did you let Max know that Clarence had kidnapped me and is taking me to Vegas?" Grace asked the three fairies who crowded around her.

"Oh, it was Myrtle," Fern started. "She wrote him a message with shaving cream."

"Until the can ran out," Myrtle said. "Then I finished with your eyeliner pencil."

"And Max believed your message?"

"He shot out of the house, on his way to the airport." Blossom pressed her hands to her heart and looked in danger of swooning.

Grace smiled, realizing she was growing awfully fond of the trio. Life would seem pretty boring when they left.

She shook herself. What was she thinking? She really must be crazy if she was lamenting their departure! The thought struck her as absurdly funny and she began to giggle.

"I'm afraid the stress is getting to her," Fern said sadly.

"It will all work out, Grace. I promise," Blossom said.

"Come on girls, let's give poor Grace a moment alone before Rat Man comes to whisk her off to Vegas."

The three godmothers, all looking at Grace with concern in their eyes, popped out of the room.

Grace continued giggling to herself, wondering which was more crazy—seeing the fairy godmothers in the first place, or missing them before they'd even left? Suddenly, despite the fact that she was a kidnapped loon, Grace felt very happy. Max was on the way. He would save her.

***

As Max rushed to his car, he admitted he'd been startled to see the word Vegas appear in the mirror, but he was astonished when the shaving cream can began to write, by itself, a message for him on the bathroom floor.

Had it been the fairy godmothers? That was the only explanation, and suddenly the thought didn't sound all that crazy to him. And if they were real, then he'd find Grace soon.

He grabbed his cell phone and dialed as he wove in and out of traffic, speeding towards the airport.

"Leo," he said when the other man answered.

"There's no new news about Grace." Leo sounded as weary as Max had felt a few moments before.

"Don't ask me to explain, because I don't think I can, but I just got a tip on Grace's whereabouts. I think she's on her way to Vegas with that Clarence guy I met at your party last night."

"Clarence?" Leo said in disbelief. "Clarence Darington? I can't see Grace leaving with that fool to go across the street, much less to Vegas"

"I don't think she went willingly. I—" He paused, wondering how to explain things without sounding crazier than Grace thought she was.

Luckily, he didn't have to explain, because Leo bellowed, "Leila!"

Leo's voice lowered as he talked into the phone. "I think I have an idea of what's going on, and I guarantee I'll be taking care of it on my end. Leila, Doris and Clarence are thick as thieves. I know the three of them were plotting to have Clarence marry Grace and take over her trust fund, but I knew Grace was too smart for them, so I didn't worry about it. Now, I suspect that either Leila or Doris or both encouraged Clarence to kidnap Grace and force her into marriage. That's the only reason I can think of for him to drag her to Vegas. It's also just the kind of stupid move the three of them would make. For pity's sake, even if Clarence did force Grace to marry him, she could divorce him the moment she got home."

Max's temper flared at the thought of Grace's so-called "family" plotting against her. No wonder she saw fairy godmothers. "Find out what they know," he told Leo.

"I plan to. Can I do anything for you?"

"Can you call the airport and take care of the ticket?" Max asked as he narrowly avoided crawling up a red Neon's tailpipe.

"Consider it taken care of. I'll call now. You just find that girl and bring her home."

"I'll do that. Thanks, Leo."

"Don't tell me thanks. If my wife put Clarence up to this, I'll take care of it. Maybe if I'd taken care of things before, this wouldn't have happened."

Leo broke off and Max heard a dial tone. "Good luck."

He snapped his cell phone back together against his thigh and put it back in his jacket pocket. Leo sounded like he really might take care of things with Leila. It should prove to be an interesting confrontation. Max was human enough to wish he could be a fly on the wall for that one.

But right now he had better things to think about. He had to jump on his charger—or plane, as it were—and save his princess from an evil toad.

Max swerved in front of a semi and shot forward. "I'm coming, Grace. Just hold on. I'm coming," he murmured, pressing the gas pedal to the floor.

He couldn't seem to move fast enough. It seemed like years to get to Vegas, instead of hours. Max got out of the cab in front of a row of hotels in Vegas and paid the driver. He'd never moved as fast as he had this morning, yet the entire day seemed to go in slow motion.

He'd rushed to the airport, barely managing to pick up his ticket and get to the terminal before take off, then had sat next to a very talkative older woman who practically swooned when he told her he was on his way to Vegas to get married.

And he was going to marry Grace as soon as he got her back in his arms. If he married her then he'd never have to let her go again. He didn't even care if she was crazy or sane, rich or poor. She was his.

As the cab drove away, Max looked at his surroundings. How on earth would he find Grace in Las Vegas? She was just one of a million people wandering beneath the bright lights and neon signs.

"I will find her," he vowed with grim determination as he walked up to the Love Nest Inn. It was a small establishment the cabbie had recommended. When Max found Grace, he didn't want to bring her back to a major casino. He wanted someplace small, quiet and intimate. Someplace special, because when he brought her back, she'd be his bride.

As he entered the quaint lobby and checked in, Max smiled. Soon Grace would be his forever.

He told the clerk, who reminded him of his grandmother, that they would stay anywhere from a day to a week, depending on how long it took him to wrap up his business.

She handed him the key and motioned the bellboy, thankfully not mentioning that his only luggage was a paper bag, which held a special purchase he'd made at the airport gift shop.

Max hurriedly followed the bellboy to room four thirty-one. When the bellboy left, he carried the paper bag into the room's pink and gold fixtured bathroom. He knew that the best way to find Grace was to ask the fairies where she was.

"Myrtle? Fern? Blossom?" he called as he opened the bag and retrieved an eyeliner pencil.

He set the pencil on the floor in front of him, as he again called, "Myrtle, Fern, Blossom? If you're here, I need your help. Vegas is a big city, and I don't have any idea where Clarence took Grace. Can you help me? I brought you an eyeliner pencil. It seemed to work better than the shaving cream."

Nothing happened. Max sat down on the cold tile floor. An hour later, the fairy godmothers still hadn't responded, despite his calling them periodically.

Heaving a frustrated sigh, Max decided he was either crazy or he'd imagined the whole thing at Grace's house. He had, after all, been up all night, pacing the floors with worry. Maybe he'd been so tired he'd hallucinated.

The explanation was sound, but Max knew it was also wrong. The fairies were real. So why hadn't they come? Were they too busy to answer him?

That possibility worried him, so he made himself think up an alternative reason for their behavior. Maybe they couldn't find him. But if that was the case, how had they found him at Grace's house?

Only one idea came to mind.

Maybe the fairies were only able to go where Grace had been. He stood and rushed into the bedroom, grabbing the phone and dialing. He didn't relish making this call, which would sound insane, but he'd do anything to save Grace, even if it meant looking like he was—what had Grace called it? Oh, yes. Sanity impaired.

"Leo?" he said when the man answered on the other end.

"Yeah, it's me. Have you found Grace?"

"Not yet. How are things going with Doris and Leila?" Max decided to start off small and work his way up to the big question.

"I was right," Leo said, his tone furious. "They intended for Grace to marry Clarence. He'd offered them a cut of Grace's money if they helped him land her. It seems they encouraged him to press his suit when you appeared on the scene last night. But you don't have to worry about them anymore." Leo's voice reduced to a growl.

"No?"

"I know I haven't always laid down the law to my wife in the past. You can ask Grace, or she's probably already told you. But Leila will not have anything more to do with Clarence. She's locked herself in her room and is standing by the door screaming at me. You see, I went into her wallet and cut up all her charge cards. It's a worse fate than a beating as far as Leila's concerned.

"On Monday she's going to start working for me. That way I can keep an eye on her, and I'm going to make her pay for her own purchases. I'm afraid I've done Grace a disservice by not putting my foot down years ago. Leila and Doris have been brutal to her on occasion, but last night wasn't just brutal..."

"Leo?" Max cut him off.

"Yeah?"

"I'm glad you've taken care of Leila, but did she tell you where Clarence was taking Grace?"

"She didn't know anything more than you did. Clarence was taking her to Vegas for a quickie wedding. He didn't want to risk you coming between him and all that lovely money."

Max sighed. He'd hoped Leila would know exactly where Clarence had planned to take Grace. Since she didn't, Max had no choice but to let his newfound friend think he was nuts.

"Leo," he said, "I have to ask one more favor."

"Anything. I feel responsible for this whole mess. It's not that I think Clarence would hurt Grace. I don't think he has it in him, but—"

"This isn't your fault, Leo, and what I'm going to ask you will sound strange. It may work and it may not, but either way I'm asking you to give me your word that you'll never tell a living soul about this."

"You've got it. Now, tell me what you want me to do."

He asked Leo to go to Grace's apartment, telling him to call as soon as he got there so Max could finish giving him his instructions.

"I feel like James Bond," Leo said, a hint of his old joviality in his voice.

Twenty minutes Leo called and said, "Okay, I'm here. Now what?"

"Go in the bathroom with the cordless phone." There was a long pause, and Max asked, "Are you there, Leo?"

"I'm walking into the bathroom right now. What is this mess all over the floor?"

"It's a long story, and I promise Grace and I will fill you in later. Right now I want you to yell, *'Myrtle, tell me exactly where Grace is.'* You got that?"

"You want me to yell *what*?" Leo choked out.

"*Myrtle, tell me exactly where Grace is.* You can ad-lib. Tell her Vegas is a big city, and Max doesn't know where to look. Tell her you're on the phone with me and will tell me what she says. Tell her we need to know *now*."

Leo hesitated, but finally called, "Myrtle, Max needs to know exactly where in Vegas Grace is. He's in his hotel room—"

"Tell her I've been trying to call her, but no one answered."

"Max says he's been calling you, but no one answered, so he sent me over here to contact you. Where's Grace?"

"Is anything happening?" Max asked urgently.

"No," Leo said.

"Well, keep calling," Max encouraged him.

"Max, I know you're a psychiatrist, but don't you think this is a little...well, crazy?"

"I know it seems that way, Leo, but it really isn't. Please keep trying."

"Myrtle?" Leo called again. "I don't think whatever's supposed to happen is going to happen," Leo said after another fifteen minutes of yelling. His voice sounded hoarse.

"Just a few more minutes," Max pleaded.

"Holy shit!" Leo's voice exclaimed over the phone.

"What is it?" Max asked, excited.

"The eyeliner pencil that was in the middle of all the ooze on the floor... Well, you won't believe this, but its writing all by itself!"

Max could hear the panic in Leo's voice. "Don't worry, Leo. I believe you because it's Grace's godmothers doing the writing. They won't hurt you. They're just trying to tell us how to find Grace."

There was a long stretch of silence. "What does it say, Leo?" Max finally asked.

"Amazing Grace Wedding Chapel." There was a quiver in Leo's voice. "Max, are you sure I'm not crazy?"

"Tell you what. If you are then I helped drive you there, so I'll treat you—no charge."

"Thanks." Leo's voice was a little stronger. "You are going to explain this all to me when you two come home, right?"

"I'll explain it as best I can," was Max's non-committal response.

"Ah. I see. You don't understand it, either."

"Not really, but I'll tell you what I can, and Grace will fill in what she can. But right now, I'm out of here," Max said, as he frantically flipped through the phone book.

"Good luck," Leo called.

"Thanks, I think I'm going to need it."

***

"He's on his way, dear," Fern told a distraught Grace.

"Yeah, yeah, yeah. That's what you told me when Clarence

hauled me onto the plane," Grace grumbled. She shifted on the bed. She was in a honeymoon suite, waiting for Clarence to come back, waiting for Max to come rescue her, waiting, just waiting.

"Max was right behind you," Blossom protested. "You have no idea how hard we worked to rearrange the schedules of a pretty major airline to get him here on time."

"So why isn't he here?" Grace was tired. She hadn't been able to sleep, what with being kidnapped and crazy. Even if she could have slept, first the godmothers had kept popping in and out of the plane, and now in and out of the hotel room, driving her even crazier with their happy chatter.

She took back every thought of missing them. She wanted this over so they'd be gone. "If Max left right around the same time I did, what's taking him so long?"

Grace closed her eyes, wishing the tacky honeymoon suite would go away. An actual red, heart-shaped bed was the centerpiece in the gaudy room. Mirrored ceiling and heart-shaped hot tub rounded out the perks. It was tacky and very red.

Clarence, the deranged snake, still expected her to marry him. He kept threatening to try his friend's concoction on her. She kept agreeing to be compliant because, according to the fairies, Max was on his way.

But there was still no Max in sight, and Grace sat in her wedding finery. The white dress the fairies and Glinda had made was to act as a wedding gown. It was topped by a veil that Clarence had produced.

Where is Max? Grace wondered, starting to panic. She knew, even if Clarence didn't, that she could get out of a marriage she'd been forced into, but she didn't want the hassle. She didn't want to spend one more minute in Clarence's slimy company. She wanted to go home. Even more than that, she wanted Max.

No, that wasn't quite right. *Want* wasn't a strong enough word to describe the feelings she had been having.

She needed him. She missed him, for a thousand different reasons. There was the way he listened to her, really listened, as if what she had to say mattered. She missed the way he smiled.

And the way he touched her. She closed her eyes, shutting out everything but the memory of Max's touch. Oh, how she missed how he touched her.

Wanted. Needed. Missed. None of the words were wrong, but none described the fullness of what she was feeling.

Love. It was the only word that fit.

She was in love with the man she'd only met two days ago. The thought was staggering and yet so simple. *I love Max!*

"Gracey?"

She realized three fairies were sitting on the bed, studying her. "Were you all reading my mind again?" she asked. Love? The feeling was too new to share, even with the fairies. She wanted time to explore the depth of the love she was feeling before she told them.

"You asked us not to," Fern reminded her.

Fern's statement didn't really answer her question, but Grace let it ride, too awed by the feeling to be annoyed, even with the fairies.

"You see, we had another little problem," Blossom said, interrupting Grace's profound revelation.

Grace's awe was replaced by renewed panic. "A little problem? Where the three of you are concerned, there's no such thing as a *little* problem. Do you remember Pauline and Terry? You had her dress up like a man to investigate that gambling ring. When Terry met her and started having feelings for her, he started worrying about his masculinity. Of course she couldn't tell him she wasn't a man without blowing her cover. And Pauline had no way of knowing that Terry was investigating the group for the Attorney General's office, because they weren't just into illegal gambling, but they were also trafficking drugs.

"You three had those two running in circles for the whole book." Grace flopped face down on the tacky bed.

She wanted to bury her face in her hands, but they were still tied. "I'm doomed!"

Myrtle reached out and raised Grace's chin. When Grace looked at her, she said, "I think you're being highly unfair, Grace.

After all, things worked out in the end. Pauline and Terry got married, and they've formed their own detective agency."

"They call it *Finders, Keepers*," Fern said excitedly. The characters had been named Pauline Finder and Terrence Kept. Grace didn't want to, but she couldn't help falling once again for her godmothers' update on characters she'd invented.

Deciding that, if she was going to be crazy she might as well go all the way, she said, "Oh, that's nice. Do they have any children?"

Fern nodded. "Almost. Pauly is pregnant. The two of them are arguing fiercely. Terry wants her to stay home, and she wants to continue working."

"He says it's too dangerous," Blossom added.

"And she says if it's too dangerous for her, because she's almost a mother, it's too dangerous for him, the father," Fern added.

Myrtle smiled and patted Grace's cheek. "Don't worry, dear. They'll work out their differences, just like you and Max will get over this kidnapping thing. All of you will be stronger for it in the end."

Stronger? Grace didn't care about being stronger, she just wanted Max. "Why isn't Max here yet?"

"Well, you see... Uh, Fern?" Blossom started, but obviously chickened out. "It's like this. Um, Myrtle will tell you."

Myrtle glared at her two faint-hearted sisters. "You see, Grace, the three of us are tied to you, and only you. We can go any place you've been, but we can't track Max. He's not our godchild, you are. So you see we, ah... Well, we lost him."

"You lost him?" Grace yelled.

Clarence came rushing into the room. "Is everything okay, Grace?" His gaze fell on her hands, apparently making sure she was still tied.

"Is everything okay? *Okay*?" Grace began to laugh hysterically.

She ran through the list of the things that were not okay. She was crazy; she was kidnapped; she was being haunted by inept fairy godmothers; and a crazy man wanted to marry her for her money.

But the worst thing in her whole list of complaints was that Max was out there looking for her, and there was nothing she could do about it. Myrtle, Fern and Blossom had lost the man she loved. She was going to be their first failure.

"Just get out of here Clarence. I don't want to see you now."

A look of understanding crossed the little weasel's face. "It's all right, dear, I understand. Pre-wedding jitters. But once my ring is on your finger, and the license is all signed and legal, then you'll feel a lot better."

"Better?" Grace scoffed, wishing she could throw something at the money grubbing rat. "Get out of here Clarence before I do something desperate."

Clarence left.

"Now," Grace began, returning her attention to the fairies. "You three tell me how it is you lost the man I love."

"Now, Grace, we lost him, but he found us," Fern explained without, of course, explaining anything.

"Could one of you please say something that makes sense!"

Myrtle held up a hand, silencing her two sisters. "It's like this. Max got on the plane, but we forgot to watch where he went from there, so we couldn't find him. Do you have any idea how big a city Las Vegas is?"

Grace nodded, unwilling to say anything that would interrupt Myrtle's train of thought.

"Well, we didn't want to worry you."

"But we were worried," Fern threw in.

"Very worried," echoed Blossom.

Myrtle glared at the two. They sat on the end of the bed and shut their mouths. Myrtle picked the story back up. "Well, we were worried. We couldn't let Max know where Clarence took you if we couldn't find him. But then Max—who we're happy to tell you is every bit as bright as we'd hoped—thought to send Leo to your house."

"Into your bathroom," Fern added.

"And I wrote the message this time," Blossom said proudly.

"Which was?" Grace asked.

Myrtle jumped back in. "Why, that Clarence is taking you to the Amazing Grace Wedding Chapel. We told Max a few minutes before we came here, so he should meet you there." The three ladies were smiling, pleased that things were coming together.

"The Amazing Grace Wedding Chapel?" Grace couldn't help laughing as relief poured through her body. Max was on his way.

Fern sighed, dreamily. "We saw it in the yellow pages when Clarence was looking through the listings, and we knew -"

"Oh, yes we knew—" Blossom echoed.

"That it was the place, the only place for you two to get married!" Myrtle exclaimed, triumphant.

"For Clarence and me to get married?"

"No, dear. You and Max," three voices said together.

"So, my white knight is really charging to my rescue?" Grace felt slightly uneasy. Something felt wrong about the fairies' explanation, but she couldn't figure out what bothered her.

"Isn't that what you wanted, Grace?" A worried wrinkle marred Myrtle's brow.

"I'm not sure," Grace mused. "It sounds so romantic in my books to have the hero charge in and save the damsel in distress. But I don't know if I want to walk around for the rest of my life knowing I had to rely on Max to save me, that I wasn't smart enough or capable enough to save myself."

"Oh, dear," three voice said, worry in their voices once again. Before Grace could ask what was wrong, they blinked out of the room.

"Wait!" she called after them. "You can't leave."

There was no use yelling, the room was empty. The fairies had left because she'd told them she didn't want Max to rescue her. She would have slapped her forehead if her hands weren't still bound. She'd told the fairies she wanted to rescue herself. She didn't have the foggiest idea how to go about it.

What had she done?

EIGHT

Max flew from the hotel, a sense of urgency riding his heels. Still dressed in his now sorry-looking tux, he hailed a taxi. "I need to get to the Amazing Grace Wedding Chapel," he told the driver as he climbed into the car.

"Ah, Amasin' Grace," the driver said in heavily accented English.

"Yes, the Amazing Grace Wedding Chapel," Max repeated, more slowly this time.

"Si, si, I will take you." The driver pushed the gas pedal to the floor. They sped into the line of traffic, cars honking as they braked to allow the taxi into the flow. The cabbie drove at an astounding speed down the street, and all the red lights turned to green as they approached.

Maybe the fairies are helping me, Max thought with a smile.

After the first fifteen minutes passed, the car gave no indication of slowing down. They also didn't seem to be any closer to their destination. Max's confidence in the fairies' help was crumbling, particularly when he remembered how their "help" had ended in the book he'd read.

"Sir?" he called to the cab driver. "Are we almost there?"

"Si, si," the man yelled back.

Max settled back in the seat and tried not to worry. But when ten more minutes went by without the cab slowing or stopping, his worry increased.

"Sir, why don't you just let me off here?" he finally asked. He'd find another cab with, hopefully, a cab driver who spoke English.

"Si, si," the cabbie called back without slowing down. They took another corner at a speed that should have tipped the vehicle over.

"Myrtle," Max yelled, knowing it probably wouldn't do any good.

"Si, si," said the cabbie.

Max had a bad feeling that this was no ordinary cab ride. *"Myrtle!"* he yelled again, not really expecting a reply. He wasn't disappointed when he didn't get one.

***

"*Myrtle*," Grace bellowed, knowing there would be no answer. What would she do now? Things were going from bad to good, from good to bad, and then from bad to worse. Why couldn't she learn to keep her mouth shut around the fairies? They took all her musings literally and, as a writer, musing was what she did best.

It looked like the godmothers planned to head Max off, so no cavalry was coming. No white knight on his giant steed would show up to rescue her. Grace MacGuire was going to have to rescue herself.

She tugged at the rope that bound her arms together, to no avail. Clarence might not be the brightest bulb in the socket, but he tied knots with a scout's dexterity.

Her white dress was beginning to nauseate her. It had been the perfect dress to wear while spending the evening with Max, but the dress didn't exist that would be perfect for any time with Clarence. She wanted out of here. She wanted Max.

She decided being a woman of the new millennium wasn't worth it. She could live with her knight riding to her rescue, but how could she convince the fairies of that?

"Myrtle, I've changed my mind," she called, only to be met with silence.

What was she going to do now?

***

"Amazing Grace Wedding Chapel," Max reminded the driver who drove erratically through the city. They were now in a section of town he thought they'd driven through before.

"Si, si," the driver placated him.

Max sat back in his seat and ground his teeth. He wanted Grace. He wanted her in his arms. He wanted to tell he loved her. He needed to tell her he knew she wasn't crazy or, if indeed she was, then he was crazy too, so it didn't matter.

He watched the buildings and scenery whizzing past. He could jump, but judging by their speed, he'd end up in the hospital and then who would save Grace?

The even-tempered Artemus Maxmillion Aaronson was feeling very out of sorts. And the focus of his out-of-sortedness was three invisible fairies who were making a muck of his relationship with Grace. If he could ever get his hands on them, he'd... He wasn't sure what he'd do, but it would be memorable, he vowed.

***

"It's time, Grace," Clarence said as he entered the room.

"Time?" She desperately tried to think of a way to stall him, but no miracle presented itself.

"Time for us to head to the chapel. I know you're excited, sweetheart. Just think, an hour from now you'll be Grace Darington. Mrs. Clarence Darington. We'll come back here, to this room, and we'll have a honeymoon."

Clarence's smile sent chills climbing Grace's spine.

"Oh, it'll be something to tell the grandkids, won't it? Then again, it's something we probably shouldn't tell them. But we'll never forget it, will we?"

"I can absolutely guarantee you that I will never forget a minute of this weekend." Grace glared at her kidnapper-would-be-husband.

He untied her hands. After so many hours behind her back, they were numb. Grace moved them awkwardly, trying to stretch them out. Each movement brought more feeling and more pain into each arm.

Clarence grimaced as he watched her restore her circulation. "I'm sorry, dear. I just didn't want to take the chance of you getting cold feet and taking off. And remember, I have that little helper in my pocket if the jitters do hit you again. One way or another, you will be my wife.

"Are you ready?" he asked, extending his hand to help her to her feet.

Grace didn't want to touch him, but she feared he would use the drug if she didn't do what he wanted.

"As ready as I'll ever be." After she stood, she continued rubbing her arms. She needed to be ready for whatever opportunities presented themselves.

"Then we're off."

"Yeah," was the best Grace could offer. How was she going to rescue herself from this man?

"Myrtle," she whispered frantically.

Who was she kidding? The fairies weren't coming to her rescue, and they weren't going to let Max come, either. It looked like Grace MacGuire's rescue rested in her own hands.

***

"Haven't we passed this casino before," Max asked the driver.

"No," the cabbie said as the cab hurtled forward faster than before.

"We really need to get to the Amazing Grace Wedding Chapel."

"Si, si," came the response.

By now, Max had lost all faith in the fairies. How was he going to get out the cab? If worse came to worse, it would eventually run out of gas. But would that happen in time to save Grace?

***

"Darling, are you happy?" Clarence said as he pulled Grace into his arms. They were riding in the back of a cab towards the wedding chapel.

An idea suddenly sprouted in Grace's head. It felt like one of those little nudges that tickled the back of her mind until it grew into a story. This particular idea was growing quickly. Clarence was the type of man who wouldn't believe that any woman could resist his charms. If she added that to his dense intelligence, her plan might work.

"Oh, Clarence, how could a girl not be happy marrying you?" she crooned, swaying toward him. "You're everything I could ever want in a husband."

He stared at her, startled. "Oh, Grace I'm so glad to hear that. I was afraid you were still stuck on that Max guy."

"How could he ever hold a candle to you? He was just a fling, a way to make you jealous. And it worked, didn't it? You couldn't stand the thought of another man marrying me, so you kidnapped me and dragged me away to make me your bride. It's all so romantic, Clarence." She wanted to throw up at the sound of her simpering voice.

"It is romantic, isn't it?" His chest visibly puffed out.

The cab stopped in front of a neon pink building that had roses planted on either side of the walkway. They dominated the front of the building, and their scent was so strong they were overpowering.

But Grace gushed, "Oh, Clarence, it's simply *darling*."

He paid the cabbie, still grasping her arm as if he feared she would bolt. "I'm glad you like it."

"Oh, I do, darling. This whole adventure has been romantic. You've swept me off my feet, carried me away to marry you, and you don't even care about my money—or my lack of it."

He chuckled. "You might not have much now, Grace, but you and I both know that you'll come into a load of it next year."

"What are you talking about?" she asked, hoping she looked puzzled.

"Darling, I know all about the trust your father set up," Clarence explained. "On your thirtieth birthday you'll have control of the entire portfolio."

Grace laughed. "Clarence, you're such a kidder. You know

that isn't true."

He abruptly halted their walk towards the front door and eyed her suspiciously. "What do you mean, it isn't true?"

"Why, you're talking about the trust as if we'll really see any of it."

"I don't understand."

"Why surely Leila and Doris told you about the codicil in my father's will?" She tried to sound nervous. "They did tell you, didn't they?"

"I'm sure they mentioned it, but why don't you tell me again?" he said as he led her to a stone bench.

She jumped into her story. "Of course, I'll tell you. Daddy couldn't stand the thought of someone marrying me for my money—or for the potential money—so he added a qualification. The money is mine, unless I marry. If I do marry, all the money will go to Daddy's favorite charity."

It was hard, but she managed not to laugh at his shocked look. If she ever stopped writing, maybe she should consider becoming an actress.

"Why didn't you tell me this before?"

Grace knew she had to play this scene just right, or Clarence would see right through her ploy. She thought about onions; she thought about every sad movie she'd ever seen; she thought about nightmares she'd had when she was a child. But none of that was enough.

She then thought of cold, endless nights without Max, and the tears began to flow. "Clarence, I thought you knew. It doesn't make a difference, does it, darling? You still want to marry me, don't you?"

Clarence didn't say a word, he just sat there staring at her, rage and disbelief warring on his face.

"Clarence?" she prodded.

"Does it make a difference?" His voice rose in volume with every word. "Of course it makes a difference, you twit! Why else would any man want to marry you?" He stood, pacing back and forth in front of her.

"You're pretty now, even beautiful, but you weren't before, and it's a sure bet you'll eventually fade back into your previous mediocrity."

He glared at her, as if her beauty was a thing to be reviled, as he continued, "You live in your books. You've never needed real human beings around. Doris and Leila have told me everything about you. They said you're a cold woman, and you'll probably be frigid in bed. So, of course, the money makes a difference."

Thinking of being held in Max's arms, Grace wanted to smile. She'd be anything but frigid then. "Clarence, I don't know what to say. I thought you loved me. I asked Max to pretend to be engaged to me just to make you jealous. I thought you loved me, and all this time you've only wanted me for my money?"

"Ah, you are a naive little thing." He smiled, as if her gullibility made him feel better about his. "I never loved you. You're right; I just wanted your money, but if there's no money..." He paused and watched her, as if waiting for her to confirm her financial status.

She did, shaking her head sadly. "There's no money."

"Well, if that's true, then I guess you and I—"

She'd fallen into the role. "Don't say it, Clarence. Please don't tell me it's over!" Dramatically, she threw her arms around his neck, clinging to him as shivers of revulsion climbed her spine.

Firmly he set her aside. "Grace, this could never work out. I need the money. You see I made certain investments on the basis of our future income. Now I don't know what I'll do." He again began to pace in front of her.

"You mean you borrowed money from some of those loan shark guys?"

"Well, not exactly. The men who fronted me the money don't deal with the normal pool-hall types. I mean they weren't loan sharks," he amended. "But they will expect their money back, and if they don't get it . . " He let the sentence die right there.

Grace felt a wave of pity sweep through her. "There must be something we can do—short of marrying, of course."

"There's nothing, unless...?"

"Yes?"

"What if we didn't get married? You'd still inherit the money, right?"

Cautiously Grace nodded her head.

"Well, maybe you'd consider loaning me the money to pay off the men I borrowed from."

"And how would you pay me back? After all, you wouldn't be my husband, and you did kidnap me and threaten to drug me."

"There was never any drug," he confessed. "I just said that to get you to cooperate. And I guess I could get a job to pay you back." He didn't sound thrilled with the idea.

"What kind of work can you do?"

"Well, I'm very good at entertaining the ladies. I make a mean martini, and I love to play baccarat."

"Not an impressive resume." Another idea occurred to her. "But I think I just might have the ideal job for you."

"What?" He narrowed his eyes suspiciously.

"A friend owns a spa in DC. He caters to older women, seeing to their needs, pampering them. With your impressive resume, you might be perfect for the job. Would you like me to call him?"

"You'd do that?" She decided Clarence might be dense, but he had enough smarts to look suspicious.

"I'll do it, but you have to promise not to kidnap women in the future. Whatever possessed you to kidnap me in the first place?" She asked the question, but she had her suspicions—three as a matter of fact.

Clarence grimaced. "I really don't know. One minute I was fuming about losing a chance with you, and the next the thought of kidnapping you just popped into my head, like magic. I'm really sorry. I hope you won't harbor any hard feelings against me."

Grace would have liked to bear a grudge, but she couldn't. It wasn't Clarence's fault. The fairies had made him do it.

"No hard feelings," she said. "At least, not too many. I'll see you after we get back to Erie and make that call to my friend."

"We?"

"Oh, Max should be here anytime now," she replied with confidence.

"How do you know?" he asked, and as she opened her mouth to tell him he shook his head. "Forget it. I don't want to know. Just like I don't want to know who you were talking to when you were alone, or how you went from an average looking woman to a knock-out."

He began to walk away from the chapel, then glanced back at her. "You'll be okay until Max comes?" he asked, seeming genuinely concerned.

"I'll be fine," she assured him.

"Just one more thing," Clarence said. Grace waited, a question in her eye. "I lied. Who were you talking to in the car and on the plane?"

"My fairy—"

Obviously he didn't like the beginning of her explanation, because he cut her off. "Never mind. I don't want to know. If Max has you committed, let me know and I'll visit. I'll even bring you your favorite candy with a nail file in it, if you like. I don't know why I did what I did, but I've underestimated you."

With that, Clarence Darington—kidnapper, would-be-husband, and a man wanted by a loan shark—jumped into a waiting cab and sped away.

Then she thought of her job offer. A job out of town, away from her and Max, that was the ticket. She doubted he'd really changed his opinion of her; he just wanted to keep himself out of trouble. But he was right about one thing, he had underestimated her.

"Is he gone, dear?" Myrtle asked, suddenly appearing in the middle of the rose garden.

"Yes, he's gone, thanks to no help from you."

"Oh, we knew you'd manage just fine. You've always been such an independent girl, and you have a good head on your shoulders. But if he's gone we'd better let Max out of that taxi cab. I think he's about ready to do that poor driver in."

With a giggle and a small *poof* Myrtle was gone.

Grace sat back down on the bench to wait for the man she loved.

***

"I know I've seen that damn casino more than once!" Max bellowed at the driver. "If you don't know where the Amazing Grace Wedding Chapel is, then let me out and I'll find a cabbie who does."

"Oh... The Amazing Grace Wedding Chapel?" the driver asked in very unaccented English. "Why didn't you say so?"

As he spoke, he made a U—turn right in the middle of the street. An oncoming semi almost landed in Max's lap, and the cabbie's foot was probably through the floor. "We'll be there in half a minute. It's only a block away."

A block away? They'd driven around in circles for so long, he was turned around, but then he saw a very familiar looking building.

"Isn't that my hotel about three blocks down that street?" he asked.

The driver looked confused for a minute. "Sir, I believe you're right, though why you bothered to take a cab when you only needed to walk four blocks, I don't know. But people are hard to figure. Why, once I had a woman hire me to drive her three doors down the block. Go figure."

The driver really did look confused as he pulled up in front of a hideous neon-pink building surrounded by roses. Max suspected that the reason he'd been driven through half of Nevada was threefold: Myrtle, Blossom and Fern.

The cabbie looked at the meter, and his confused look was replaced by shock. "Fifty-seven dollars? That can't be right. I only drove you four blocks."

Max felt sorry for the poor guy. "Don't worry about it. This was one appointment I didn't want to miss. I appreciate the ride." He tossed a very large denomination through the window.

"Girls," he said to the thin air when the cabbie drove away. "I know you did it. I don't know why, but I know it was the three of you. Grace had better be here, and she had better not be married to Clarence Whatever-his-name-is. Grace," he called, hurrying toward the ugliest, pinkest building he'd ever seen. "I'm coming."

NINE

Grace closed her eyes and waited, certain that Max was on his way. He hadn't had the opportunity to play her white knight, but there was no question in her mind that he was the man she wanted to spend the rest of her life with.

"Grace?" She sat up straight. It was Max. He ran up the walkway, a flash of black among the thousands of roses. She stood and smiled at him. Everything would be all right.

"Grace," he said again, rushing to her and pulling her into his arms. "What happened? Are you all right?"

She laughed for the sheer joy of it. Max was hugging her close, as if he feared she'd disappear again. "I'm fine. Really I am."

He held her away from him and looked her up and down. "Are you sure?"

"Positive." She pulled him to the bench next to her. "So much has happened."

"I was worried sick about you."

"So was I, at first. The fairies put some kind of spell on Clarence. The dimwit kidnapped me and brought me here to marry him. I was only annoyed at the fairies because I knew you'd come to my rescue. But then they lost you. That's when I started to worry. I thought I was a goner, but they found you. That's when I made my big mistake."

"Your big mistake?"

She nodded. "I said I wasn't sure I wanted to be rescued. I mean, it's a new millennium. A woman should be able to stand on her own two feet. The minute I voiced the thought, I wished I could suck the words right back in. The fairies took me literally, which means I had to rescue myself."

His brows rose a fraction of an inch. "That's why I spent the last hour driving around Vegas in gigantic circles with an English speaking taxi driver who only spoke Spanish?"

Grace laughed. "Yep, that's why."

"So how did you get rid of Clarence?"

"I told a big lie. I told him that if I married there would be no inheritance. That was enough to scare him off. I'm surprised you didn't meet him on the sidewalk. He just left."

"That's a shame. I really wanted to have a little talk with him about stealing my woman."

My woman. Grace liked the sound of those words. "What would you have said to him?"

"I wasn't thinking about using words. This is a case where a physical demonstration would have been better."

Grace stared at him in surprise. Sweet, humorous Max appeared able to do bodily harm—a lot of bodily harm if that ferocious look in his eyes was real.

Suddenly, his dangerous look faded, and her sweet Max was back. Gently, he wrapped her in his arms and said, "I was so worried about you."

"I was, too, at first, but when I realized the fairies set poor Clarence up, I ended up feeling sorry for the guy. I even offered to help him find a job."

"You what? Regardless of why he did it, the guy *kidnapped* you. How could you offer to help him get a job? For that matter, what kind of job do you hope to get him? From what I've seen, he doesn't look very employable."

"Oh, he's perfect for this job," Grace said, grinning impishly. "He'll be playing boy-toy for a bunch of old women. Don't you think that's punishment enough for what he did?"

"Only if one of the women is Doris."

"Oh, I think that's a delightful idea," Grace said, clapping her hands as she added another facet to her plan. "I'll make Doris a part of the deal."

"Then he'll definitely get his just reward," Max said, chuckling. "Remind me never to make you mad, okay?"

"Okay," Grace murmured, snuggling against him and savoring the feel of him. She basked in his warmth, and all the frustrations, all the fear for her sanity, all the worry about the Steps and her work faded. Being held by Max was all that mattered.

"Grace, where do we go from here. What are your plans about us?" he asked.

"Plans? About us?" she repeated breathlessly. Just being next to Max set her heart to racing. She could scarcely breathe, much less think about them.

"Yes, about us. As in, what is going to happen to us? So, where do you want to go from here?"

"You were going to make an appointment for me with your friend..."

Grace allowed the sentence to fade. She didn't want, or need, to see a psychiatrist anymore. She couldn't explain the fairy godmothers, but she *did* believe in them. If that meant she was crazy, then so be it. She didn't want anyone curing her of this particular delusion.

Max gave her a reassuring hug. "Grace, after all I've witnessed, and all we've been through since we met, there's no way I could deny that your fairies exist. It's my professional opinion you're not crazy."

"So you aren't going to send me to your colleague?"

"You're not crazy, so it isn't necessary," he said. "Now that we've settled the matter of your mental status, let's get back to my original question. What are we going to do about us?"

"I don't know. What do you think we should do?"

She looked nervous, Max decided. More nervous than she had when she'd walked into his office.

Max knew it didn't make sense, but it felt as if Grace had

been the center of his soul for his entire life. He wanted to tell her he loved her. In fact, he wanted to shout it to the world, but he was afraid it would be too much for her to handle after all she'd been through.

He gently tightened his hold on her, hoping his touch said all he couldn't say out loud yet. "I want a chance to talk about it, but not here."

"Where?" Grace asked, not that it mattered. She would follow Max anywhere. She wanted to take him by the hand and drag him into the chapel. She wanted to promise to love, honor and obey—well, she wouldn't promise to obey—but she had no doubts about the love and honor part.

Despite how much she wanted to say the words, she held off. Things were going too fast, and she needed to slow them down."I have a room," Max said. "We can—"

"No hanky panky," Myrtle said as all three fairies winked into view.

Grace gave a resigned shake of her head. They were back. It had been too much to hope they would leave her in peace. She might not want to believe they were just delusions, but she did want some time *alone* with Max. "Go away, girls. My white knight has ridden to my rescue, so your job is done."

"Not until you walk down the aisle and declare your true love." The three godmothers sat on the bench across from them.

"Max, could you excuse us a minute?"

His gaze swept the garden. "Sure. Where are they?"

"They're on the bench across from us," she said. "I need a minute to talk to them."

He rose. "I'll be just over there."

At the loss of his touch, Grace felt an almost a physical ache. She wanted to chase after him and make him hold her again, but she knew she had to take care of first things first. Three fairy godmothers needed to be taught a lesson in true magic—the magic of the pen.

"Myrtle, Fern and Blossom, we need to talk."

"Talk is what you and Max need to do," Blossom said. "Gracey, you love him. We know you do and you know you do, so tell him."

"I'm not ready to say those words to him," Grace announced, deciding it was time to let the fairies know who was running this show. She should have done it the moment they appeared in her car. Then things might have turned out differently.

But then she might not have met Max, she realized. As she recalled Max's touch, she realized she wouldn't alter the past. She would, however, take charge of her future with Max.

"What's wrong with telling Max right now?" Fern frowned, her displeasure evident.

"Right now, the only thing I'm going to declare is I'm tired. Too tired to sort this out. I need a night. One full night with no fairy interventions."

"It's our job." Myrtle's arms folded across her ample chest, daring anyone to challenge her.

Grace accepted the challenge. "Make that two nights. You're hereby taking a leave of absence. A forty-eight hour absence. Max and I want to sort things out for ourselves."

The three fairies opened their mouths, but Grace held up her hand. "Don't say a word. If you want to see this match work—and I know you do—then I must prove to myself that what I feel for Max originated from me. I have to know that it's not some magical spell you three whipped up."

"We'd never—"

"We couldn't!"

"It's against all the rules."

Grace ignored their objections. She wasn't backing down. This was too important. "Rules or not, the three of you are officially off duty for a full forty-eight hours."

"Grace, we'd be derelict in our duties—" Myrtle started.

"Or else," Grace interrupted.

Myrtle's eyes narrowed. "Or else what?"

"Or else, I—" Grace didn't need to finish the statement. The three fairies were obviously reading her mind again because their faces grew pale.

"You wouldn't!" Blossom looked ready to faint.

"If I can create three fairies, then I can write a book where the fairies lose their powers and have to live as mere mortals for one full year."

"Oh, Gracey." Fern appeared ready to cry. "What have we ever done to you?"

"Besides turn my world upside down?"

"I don't understand why you're so upset. It is going to end with a happily ever after." Myrtle looked as sick as her sisters.

"I won't know that until I have a chance to really get to know Max," Grace asserted. "That means no fairies, no bad-tempered step-family, no kidnappers, no parties. I need time. Quiet, peaceful, sane time to be sure of my feelings." She paused and softly added, "Please?"

Myrtle scowled. "Grace, you know we're not supposed to—"

"And, if I don't get that time," Grace broke in, her mind working overtime on the delicious possibilities. "I'll make it worse than just being human for a year. I could give birth to a new fairy whose one goal in life is to see you three married to humans, which would mean you would have to stay human forever."

"Oh, to think that you could be so mean!" Blossom wailed.

"We should have known after all the awful things she made us do to Nettie, Pauline and the rest." Fern shook a stern finger in Grace's face. "You're...you're warped."

"Grace," Myrtle said, her chastising tone making it evident she meant to argue.

Grace folded her arms across her chest and gave them each a hard look. "There is no discussion. I have forty-eight hours with Max. No eavesdropping or visits from the three of you. No matter what happens. Max and I will work out what happens next."

"Fine." Blossom produced a bright yellow hanky and

inelegantly blew her nose.

"You'll miss us," Fern warned.

Not ready to trust the three, Grace added, "And no peeking. Swear it."

Three hands rose in unison. "On our fairy oaths, we swear."

Before Grace could respond, they were gone in a puff of smoke.

She nervously rubbed her hands together. She had her time alone with Max, and now it was up to her, Grace MacGuire, to see if this magical feeling in her heart was fairy magic or a one-true-love fairy tale come true.

"Max?" she called.

He came back up the path. "What happened?"

"We're alone. I scared them off." The idea of turning the fairies human was still tempting. She had the Danner series to finish, but after that she could pitch the idea to her editor. A series of three books to wrap up the fairy tales.

"You're sure they're gone?" Max glanced over his shoulder. "For good?"

"We should be so lucky," Grace said dryly. "No, just for forty-eight hours. I wanted time to think without them."

"To think about what?"

Was it her imagination, or did Max look as nervous as she felt? She wasn't sure she wanted to know that answer, so she said, "To think about your question. You know, the one of what's next?"

Max led her down the path. "I think the first thing we do is get something to eat and unwind. I don't think I've ever had a couple days like these."

"And I pray you—no, *we*—never do again." Grace would definitely lose her marbles if she had to live through another fairy adventure.

***

"They're gone. They're really gone." Grace flopped on the bed in Max's room at the Love Nest Inn. It was quaint, even romantic with soft peach walls, doilies on the dressers, and lace curtains. It seemed so un-Vegas, so normal.

"What do we do first?" she asked Max.

"Eat. If you're hungry, of course," Max answered, sitting on the chair next to the bed.

"I'm starving," she admitted.

"Should we go out or stay in?"

"In. I'm so tired, I don't think I could handle a restaurant."

"Dinner it is." He picked up the phone and paused. "I just realized, I don't know what kind of food you like."

"Italian food is my favorite, but I like most anything except brussel sprouts. Can't abide those little green balls of yuck." She pulled off her pumps. Next week she'd buy some new sneakers. And jeans. She'd spent too long in her dress and heels and never wanted to get dressed up again. "I don't know your favorite food, either."

He smiled. She might not know his favorite foods, but she already relied on his smile. It warmed her through and through.

"I love Italian. Chinese, too. And I can't stand broccoli, so you can eat my broccoli, and I'll eat your brussel sprouts."

"Sounds like a good deal," she said as he dialed the phone.

Max placed their order, hung up and studied her a moment. "While you were missing I started thinking about all the things I didn't know. Now I know your favorite foods, but there's another thing that's bothered me?"

"What's that?"

"I don't know your middle name. It's stupid, I know. But it's bothered me that I didn't know it." He sat next to her on the bed. "I want to know everything about you."

Grace felt her face grow hot as she mumbled her middle name.

"What did you say?"

Her face grew warmer. "Kelly."

"Grace Kelly?" Max laughed. "It suits you."

"Is that why you're laughing at it?"

"I'm laughing because it's not what I expected." He pulled her into his arms and hugged her tight. "You're not what I expected."

"What did you expect?"

"When you came into my office, I thought you were an eccentric writer."

"I am."

"Maybe." He toyed with her pale blond hair. Weighing each strand, marveling at its texture.

"What *do* you want, Grace?"

She wanted to say, *You. I want you.* But she couldn't seem to get the words out. She settled for, "Food. I'm famished." It wasn't exactly the truth. She was starving, but for Max's touch.

"Before the food comes, we have one thing to do." He walked across the room and flipped a button on the clock radio sitting on the dresser. Jarring rock sounds tumbled through the room. Max started moving through the stations, looking for just the right one.

He stopped at a slow country song about finding love. Smiling at Grace he said, "I just realized that we never did get that slow dance at Leila's party. I'm afraid that the fairy godmothers won't like it if their Cinderella doesn't get her waltz."

He walked to Grace and extended his hand. "Would the fair lady consent to dancing with her knight?"

Grace shook her head. "The lady prefers dancing with her prince." Taking his hand, she slid into his arms. He moved them in an easy rhythm, swaying to the music. Grace had never been much of a dancer, but this once—this one very special dance—she felt like she was the most graceful woman to ever put her feet on a dance floor.

While Max whirled her around the room, Grace drank in the scent of him. Even after spending more than twenty-four hours in his tux, he still smelled good. He looked good, too. Maybe the fairies were still weaving their magic, or maybe it was just that Grace and Max were weaving their own spell. Whatever it was, Grace knew that she'd never been anywhere that felt as right as being held in Max's arms.

I love him. She rolled the words around on her tongue, and then rolled them around in her heart. It wasn't just a fairy-feeling, of that she was sure. She loved Max's humor, his ability to believe in her, and in the godmothers whom he couldn't see. She loved Max's need to take care of her, but she wanted a chance to take care of him as well.

Yes, she definitely loved him. So how should she tell him? Would he believe her, or would it scare him off?

The song ended and he kissed her. It was a slow, easy kiss that she never wanted to end.

When Max let her come up for air, she said, "Max, I lied when I said I wanted food."

Huskily, he asked the question she'd been asking herself. "Then what do you want, Grace?"

"You." The moment she said the word, she knew the others would come easily. "I've wanted you since the moment I saw you. I worried that it might be my mental decline or the fairies working some charm. But, while Clarence had me, I realized it was more than that." She hesitated.

"You wanted me?"

"More. I know it's probably too soon to say this, but I love you, Max."

He opened his mouth to speak, and she placed a finger over his lips. "Shh. Let me finish. I know all the reasons for waiting to say the words. It's too soon. I've been on shaky mental ground, and I'm sure there are other reasons. But I don't care about all the reasons. I love you."

She trailed her hands down his shirt front, fumbling with the buttons. "Let me show you."

"You're sure about this Grace?"

"More sure than I've been of anything in my life."

Feeling as bold as one of her characters, Grace slowly tugged Max's shirt out his pants and finished unbuttoning it. Boldly, she ran her fingers down his chest, toying with the downy hair covering it. "You feel so good."

"My turn," he murmured, working at the small buttons holding the fairy dress in place. "Have I mentioned how stunning you look in this dress?"

"Maybe once or twice, but a woman doesn't mind hearing those things frequently."

Max unbuttoned the last button and slipped the dress from her shoulders. It fell to the floor, pooling at her feet. "Would you like me to mention how good you look out of it?"

"Oh, I think that's fine, too," she answered breathlessly.

His fingers traced her shoulder blade. That one small touch let loose a torrent of desire within her.

"Grace, are you really sure?" Max asked her. He needed her to be sure, because with each passing minute the idea of stopping became more difficult to entertain. Max wanted her—needed her—in his arms more than he'd ever needed anything in his life.

"Yes, Max, please."

It was all the prompting he needed. Max lowered Grace to the bed, unleashing all his pent-up needs. He touched and tasted and teased her with his hands and his lips, driving her to the edge. He took possession of her, and marveled as she fell over that edge, pulling him over with her.

Holding her, Max buried his face in her hair and knew with a certainty that this was where he was meant to be. Grace MacGuire was the woman he was meant to be with for the rest of his life.

***

A touch pulled at Grace, drawing her from her fantasy dreams of a man who... Her eyes flew open. *A man who was in bed next to her, stroking her back.* Hazy with sleep, Grace's body warmed at the thought of Max's and her night together. They'd made love, then eaten, then made love again.

"Good morning," Max said. "Actually, good afternoon."

"What time is it?" She rolled over and faced him, gently touching her lips to his.

"Almost lunch." He casually moved a stray strand of hair off her forehead.   "Are you hungry for lunch, Grace Kelly MacGuire?" Laughter danced in his eyes.

"You're not mocking my name, are you?"

"Never."   The promise sounded less than believable, especially when he started to chuckle.

Grace grabbed a pillow from under her head. "You realize that this means war, don't you?"

He sat up and inched away. "Pillow fights are juvenile."

"Well, for your information, Dr. Artemus Maxmillion Aaronson, I'm occasionally a little juvenile when it comes to revenge."

"Grace," he said in warning.

"What?" she asked innocently a second before soundly thumping his head with the pillow. "My mother happened to like Grace Kelly."

Max dove at her, pushing her down to the mattress and pinning her arms at her sides. "I like your name and I swear I won't mock it again."

She was so close, so tempting, Max couldn't help leaning down and giving her a proper good morning kiss. When he finally eased his lips from hers, he flopped back onto the bed and pulled her into his arms. "You know, when I couldn't find you, it bothered me that I didn't know your middle name. There's still so much we don't know about each other. You haven't even met my family yet."

"You've never told me about your family, not that there's been much time for that kind of talk." She snuggled closer to him.

"My family?" Max said distractedly. Her wiggling was making him nuts. "Well, Mom and Dad are still alive, and they live in Florida."

"I'd like to meet them." Grace wiggled a little closer.

"That can be arranged," Max murmured, nibbling at her shoulder.

"Brothers and sisters?"

"One each," he managed between nibbles. "Nick and Joy. I'm the oldest, then Nick, then Joy."

Grace put a hand on his chest. "First we finish the discussion. The purpose of this fairyless time is to get to know each other, and I've got to admit, I'm curious. You know about my family, such as it is. I want to know about yours. Start with their full names. After all, you might laugh at Grace Kelly, but, in the bizarre department, I don't think it begins to touch Artemus Maxmillion. How about it? Joy and Nick?"

"Delphina Joy and Osborn Nicholas. Mom and Dad wanted to name us all after our grandparents." Grace giggled and Max nipped her shoulder.

"Ow."

"Don't mock our names. We all decided we were glad there wasn't another girl Artemus and Delphina were Dad's parents, and Osborn and Clementine, were Mom's. Clementine Aaronson? What a nightmare that would have been."

Grace was giggling now. "Well, I guess your family reunion is the one place my name won't stand out."

"That was a rotten thing to say." He silenced her, devouring her lips, memorizing her body with his touch.

"Before this goes any further..." he paused.

"What?" she whispered.

"I just want to check. Myrtle? Fern? Blossom?" he called. No fairies answered, but then he never heard them anyway. "Did you hear anything?" he asked.

"Nope," Grace said, a Cheshire Cat-like smile on her lips. "I think I put the fear of my pen in them."

"*Damn*, you're a good writer."

***

Max stepped out of the shower, dreading climbing back into his tux. It was bad enough to have to wear one for a couple hours at a party, but now he'd been wearing the thing since Saturday and it was Monday.

Instead of finding a tux hanging on the back of the door

where he'd left it, he found a crisp new pair of jeans and a soft blue t-shirt. Sitting on the counter were a pair of boxer shorts, a pair of white tube socks, a toothbrush and toothpaste. A pair of Nike sneakers were on the floor.

"The fairies have struck again," he called out to Grace.

She walked into the bathroom clad in jeans and a soft pink shirt. "Oh, you've already found the clothes. Well, it wasn't Myrtle, Fern or Blossom this time. It was me. I don't know about you, but climbing into that gown—even though I love it—wasn't appealing, so I got us new outfits."

"How did you manage that?"

"I bribed the bell boy to run to a department store after you went to sleep last night," she told him. "He brought them up with breakfast or, rather, lunch." Grace had enjoyed ordering the *non-manhunting* clothes.

"So, no fairies are involved?"

"No fairies. At least not for a while." They had the day to be with one another. A day to themselves. A day to play, to learn about each other, and then they'd have the night. Grace smiled. Another night with Max might not be just what the fairies ordered, but it was just what Grace longed for.

"What are we going to do today?" she forced herself to ask. If she kept thinking about another night with Max, they'd never leave the hotel room.

"Have you ever been to Vegas?"

Grace shook her head. "I'm not much of a gambler."

"We could see a show."

"I'd like that." She would have agreed to do anything, as long as Max was with her.

"Let's go down and ask the concierge. He can point us at something good."

After the show they'd played a few slots. Then they'd eaten a romantic dinner at a small Italian restaurant which wasn't part of the glitzy casinos. In the candlelight, they'd talked of family, of themselves, of pasts and present. The only thing they hadn't discussed was their future. Grace wasn't sure what would happen tomorrow when the fairies returned, or when she and Max returned to Erie and the real world, but she refused to worry. For this one perfect moment, Max was hers. She wasn't going to waste an instant of it.

Max had been gracious enough to let Grace pick the show. It wasn't until they returned to their room that night that he teased, "Donny Osmond?"

Donny had been Grace's childhood fantasy, and she couldn't pass up the opportunity to see him. "Yes, Donny Osmond. You liked his show, and you know you did."

"I liked watching you like his show," Max corrected. "I thought you were going to pass out when he sang 'Puppy Love.'"

"That was my favorite song when I was in grade school." One of the highlights of her childhood was her first concert, when Donny Osmond and his brothers danced onto the stage. "He was so cute. Still is."

"Should I be jealous?"

"Let me reassure you."

Grace pushed him back toward the bed, and they tumbled into it. Then Grace set about demonstrating every way she could that she loved him. Max was tender and gentle with her, but the words of love she murmured over and over to him weren't returned.

It was too soon, she kept telling herself. But, try as she might, she wasn't sure she believed it. The scope of her feelings for him were overwhelming.

Max might enjoy her, might not think she was crazy anymore, but Grace was beginning to wonder just how he felt about her. She had told him she loved him. He had seemed to welcome the words, but he hadn't echoed them.

He was a tender lover, but she wanted more. What if she never got more? What if the fairies were wrong?

What if Max didn't love her?

Wouldn't it be ironic if they'd found her the man of her dreams, but hadn't managed to find Max the woman of his?

TEN

"Max, I feel ridiculous," Grace said the next morning. "Can't I take this blindfold off?"

They sat in the back of a taxi, and Max had blindfolded Grace. She'd thought they'd leave for home first thing, but Max had announced he had something special he wanted to do with her.

"Grace, I keep telling you this is a surprise," Max said.

Grace had made another discovery about Max. He was stubborn. She sighed and relaxed in the seat until the taxi stopped.

"We're here."

"Where's here?"

"You're not the patient sort, are you? Just sit still a minute."

"No, I'm not patient and I feel foolish. Can't I take the blindfold off?"

"No." After paying the driver, Max helped her from the car and steered her as she walked. "We're almost there."

The overpowering smell of roses gave their location away. "Max? We're back at the chapel?"

He pulled the blindfold from her eyes. "Have a seat." They were directly in front of the bench where she'd waited for him. "There's one last thing we have to do before we go home."

"What's that?" she whispered, grateful to be sitting since her knees suddenly felt very weak.

Max sank to one knee. "Grace, will you marry me?"

She stared at him mutely, aware that it wasn't the most romantic response, but unable to form a coherent sound. She'd worried that he hadn't said he loved her, and yet, here he was proposing. Could it mean that he did indeed feel the same way about her?

Max took her hand in his. "It seems to me that there could be no place on Earth more appropriate for us to marry then in the Amazing Grace Wedding Chapel.

"We're already in Vegas," he continued, "and I want this more than I've ever wanted anything in my life."

"You're sure?" she finally managed to ask.

"Grace, I love you. It happened so fast, but I know I love you and no amount of time will change my feelings."

Tears gathered in her eyes. "You love me? I thought...when you didn't say the words, I worried that maybe the fairies were wrong." Her voice dropped to a whisper. "I thought maybe you wanted me, but just couldn't love me."

He cocked his head, his brow creased. "Of course I love you."

"You didn't say so."

"Grace, I'm so sorry. This is so new to me and, and that's no excuse. I was waiting to tell you, then we made love and I thought you knew and--" He stopped. "Grace Kelly MacGuire, I love you more than words can say. It has nothing to do with fairy godmothers, nothing to do with time. It's just there. You're a piece of me I never knew existed until you walked into my office. You just slid right into that hole in my heart and filled it with love."

"But should we really get married today?" She wanted it more than she'd ever wanted anything, but Grace needed to know Max felt the same way. "We could wait."

Max shook his head. "I love you. You love me. Waiting won't change that."

It was the truth. She loved him, and there wasn't anything she wanted more in the world than to marry him. "Yes, I'll marry you." Her heart felt ready to explode with happiness. She couldn't help recalling that the first time the fairies had appeared in her car they'd told her that her perfect world wasn't quite so perfect. Looking at Max, she acknowledged they were right.

She glanced at her watch. It was almost time for the fairies to return. "Girls?" she called out. "Are you coming to the wedding?"

"We wouldn't miss it."

"You bet your life we're coming."

"Do you know how much work we invested in this relationship? Of course we'll be there," humphed the three sisters, one on top of another.

"Well, then come on," Grace called.

Max looked at her questioningly. "Are they coming to the wedding?"

"Yes. They assure me they wouldn't miss it."

"Then I want to say something to the three of you." Max faced the direction in which Grace had been speaking. "You've put the two of us through hell these last few days. If I could see you, I'd probably throttle you all. But since I can't, I guess I'll just say thank you, because despite the problems, you've given me the greatest gift I've ever received."

Three fairy godmothers—one dressed in buttercup yellow, one in moss green and one in sunset red—sniffed, wiping their respective noses with color coordinated handkerchiefs. One by one they filed out of the rosebushes and tip-toed up to plant a kiss on Max's cheek.

"Did they just kiss me?" Max asked Grace, gently rubbing his tingling cheek. She nodded, sniffing too. "Well, thanks girls. Now, come on inside, 'cause we're going to a wedding!"

The inside of the chapel was as syrupy as the outside. Every surface was painted pink and red, and roses abounded. The Reverend John Smith presided. In the sing-song chant of the old time chaplains he asked, "Do you, Artemus Maximillion Aaronson, take Grace Kelly MacGuire to be your lawfully wedded wife?"

Max's "I do," rang loud and clear.

"And do you, Grace Kelly MacGuire, take Artemus Maximillion Aaronson to be your lawfully wedded husband?"

"I do."

"She does," rang out three other voices at the same time. The fairies, standing directly behind Grace, rested their hands on her shoulders.

Grace turned and smiled at them. They'd been right in the car, her life had been missing something, or rather someone. Her gaze turned to Max. "I do," she whispered again.

"You may now exchange rings."

Max looked sick.

"He forgot the rings," Myrtle whispered.

"Ah, Grace?" Max said.

"Tell him to check his pocket," Fern added.

"Feel in your pocket," Grace whispered.

"The right one." Blossom pointed.

Max reached into the right pocket and withdrew a black jewelry box. Two plain gold bands sat snugly inside its velvet interior.

He leaned toward Grace and whispered, "The fairies?"

"The fairies," she whispered back, smiling. "Is it big enough to prove—"

Max cut her off. "There was nothing left to prove. If I hadn't believed when the shaving cream can wrote me that message, I certainly would have when I found myself standing here. This is a dream come true."

Grace blushed and nodded to the confused looking Reverend to continue.

"With this ring I thee wed..." he intoned. The bands fit perfectly on their respective fingers. Grace and Max beamed at each other as the Reverend said, "Then by the power vested in me by the state of Nevada, I now pronounce you man and wife. You may kiss the bride." And, like a man denied food for much too long, Max's lips plundered Grace's until finally the Reverend cleared his throat.

"Um," Grace murmured, a flood of warmth invading her cheeks.

"Sorry," Max apologized for the both of them.

"Ah, yes. Well, congratulations," said the Reverend as he hustled them to a table at the back of the chapel to sign the necessary papers. "It's nice to join together couples who obviously love each other as much as you two do," he told them. "Working in this business, you get to know which couples have a chance and which will be back next year for a quickie divorce."

"And which are we?" Grace couldn't stop herself from asking.

"Neither."

"Neither?"

"You two are the rarest sort. You're what we call a sure thing. If I were a horse-racing man, I'd say you were going to make it to the finish line way ahead of the rest, no problem."

Grace blushed again; she couldn't help herself. This was all too new and wonderful. "Amen to that."

"I think it's time we left," Max said, hugging his wife close to his side after tucking their precious papers into his pocket.

"I think so, too." Grace was suddenly nervous and shy.

"Thank you," they both called as they left the rose festooned church.

"Congratulations," the Reverend called back.

As they reached the rose garden a quiet voice called, "Grace."

"Max, the fairies are calling me," Grace told her new husband. Husband--how she loved that word already. "I want to go tell them goodbye."

"I'll wait here," he said, sensing her need to bid the fairies a private farewell.

"Thank you," she said, kissing his cheek.

"Tell them I said thank you and give them all a kiss from me," he said and moved toward the street.

Grace walked into the center of the garden, an open space surrounded by benches, with a small fountain—naked Cupid included—bubbling merrily.

"We just wanted to say goodbye," Blossom sniffed.

"And apologize for all the grief we put you through," Fern chimed in.

"Really, an apology isn't necessary," Grace said. "You've done so much for me. I don't have any idea how to even begin to thank you. You were right. My life was missing something; it was missing Max."

As she spoke, tears streamed down her face. As much trouble as they'd been, she would miss them. Things were going to be a little too normal, a little too flat, without their friendly banter and their incessant popping in and out.

"Now, now, now. Just look at all of us," Myrtle sniffed. "Crying like we'll never see each other again."

"I'll be seeing more of you?" Grace asked.

"Of course you will," Myrtle said.

"You have the book series you're working on, so you'll see us there. And
you might want to think about letting us do a few things right instead of
constantly bumbling. Just look at how well we handled your romance."

Grace just stared at the eldest of her fairy godmothers.

"Well," Myrtle admitted. "It all ended up right, and that's all that matters in the end."

"You're right, Myrtle. It ended up better than right. It ended up perfect, and I have the three of you to thank for that." One by one, she hugged the fairy godmothers. "Thank you all."

"You're welcome," said Fern.

"No problem," said Blossom.

"Well, we couldn't have you wandering around trying to find romance on your own," Myrtle said, smiling. "You've helped us with so many couples, and there are a few more out there we're meant to help. Anyway, we couldn't just see you bumping around on your own anymore. You mean too much to us."

"So, this isn't goodbye. We'll be seeing you," Myrtle promised.

"Soon," Blossom said.

"Very soon," Fern echoed.

The fairies had found her her-own-true-love. What else could they have up their communal sleeves? "What are you going to do now?"

"Well..." said Blossom. "We just received our newest orders. It seems that Max's sister Joy—"

"It seems," Fern continued, "that poor Joy isn't very joyful."

"And we've found this perfectly wonderful man who needs a wife desperately, only he might not appear perfect right away. He has a little girl who needs someone to love her, and we think Joy would be a perfect stepmother," Blossom finished.

"So don't you worry about what we'll be doing. We will see you soon. Now go take care of your husband," Myrtle ordered, and as easily as that, the fairies were gone. The quickness of their departure after so much time trying to get rid of them left Grace feeling uneasy, at least until Max walked up the path.

"Is it okay if I tell them thanks again?" Max asked.

She missed the three fairies already.

"We're never far away," Myrtle whispered, reading her mind one last time, but not appearing.

"Sorry. It's too late," Grace told her husband. Her husband. Her heart swelled at the thought.

"I guess you're right," Max said, pulling his wife into his arms. "It was too late for me the minute you walked into my office. Have I told you yet today that I'm crazy about you?"

"No, I don't think you mentioned it," Grace said, laughing. "But it's okay. I'm absolutely mad about you."

"I know," Max said as he looped his arm over her shoulder and led her toward their future.

***

"Well, that's done," Fern said as they watched Grace and Max leave.

"Not until we say the words," Blossom reminded her.

Together the three fairy godmothers said, "And they lived happily ever after."

And Grace and Max did live happily ever after. But poor Joy... Never mind, that's another story.

One

"Joy."

Joy paused and looked behind her. The only thing that met her eye was an empty room. Despite the chills climbing up her spine, she forced herself to return to her unpacking.

All day long she'd felt like she was being watched, which was absurd. Who on earth would want to watch her? She gave a little laugh. No one. That was the answer. She was boringly normal— five-foot- three inches of well-padded normalcy— not the type of woman to inspire anyone to follow her. No chestnut curls or azure eyes. Nope. Just straight brown hair and blue eyes. Normal. No secret admirers, no stalkers; not for Joy Aaronson.

"Joy."

She jumped and whirled around. This time the room wasn't empty. Three elderly ladies stood side-by-side, watching her. No, not just watching, they were studying her. Joy's mouth was suddenly as dry as the Sahara, and the chills blew Arctic against her backbone. "I'm sorry, you must have the wrong room."

The trio smiled in unison. It might have been endearing if the entire situation wasn't so eerie. She hadn't heard the door open, hadn't heard a sound.

In the blink of an eye, Joy took in her uninvited guests. They were small women, smaller than Joy herself. None of them could be over four and a half feet tall. They were in their mid-fifties, Joy would guess. One was a redhead, who sported a sequined red dress and stiletto heeled shoes that belonged on someone thirty years the woman's junior. The next was a brunette, who wore a green orient inspired dress. The last was a blonde, whose hair was a hideous shade of yellow that belonged on a canary, not on a human. She wore a buttercup gown that would have looked at home on Scarlet O'Hara.

The trio was as extraordinarily different as Joy was ordinary to the point of boring. Even at their ages, they were the types who might attract a stalker.

"The maid showed me up to this room, so I'm pretty sure I'm in the right one. You might want to check with her. She'll be able to point you all in the right direction." Joy smiled sympathetically. There was no use alienating the weird trio when she planned to beg favors from them later.

"Joy, we're not in the wrong room by mistake," said the brunette.

"We don't make mistakes," said the blonde. The redhead shot her a funny look and the blond hastily added, "Well, not often." The redhead raised another eyebrow. "Okay, maybe we make mistakes, but they turn out right in the end. And we're not mistaken about the room, or who's in it. We're looking for you."

"Girls, I suggest you allow me to make our introductions." The redhead was obviously accustomed to taking charge. "Joy, we know about Ripples, and that's one of the reasons we're here, to see to it this fundraising party is successful."

Joy felt a surge of pride. Ripples was her baby, a non-profit foundation that funded a number of small charities. She'd realized years ago that she couldn't change the world, but Ripples was her attempt to change a small corner of it.

"Ripples can use all the friends, and all the help with fundraising we can get." Raising money for Ripples was the reason Joy was attending this upscale house party, and though she welcomed their help, something about these three women still made her nervous. "I'm glad Mrs. St. John has already started to spread the word about Ripples and what we do."

"Actually, she didn't. At least not that we know of. You see, we're friends of your brother Max. Actually we knew Grace first, but we've come to know and love Max as well."

Joy sank to the bed, blatantly staring at the three. Friends of Grace? Grace was a romance author who wrote about three bumbling fairy godmothers. Godmothers who - now that Joy stopped and thought about it - these women were dressed exactly like. A simple explanation occurred to her.

"Is this party a costume one? How wonderful of you to dress up like Grace's fairy godmothers. Did Trudi tell you I was coming? If everyone's costume is as great as yours, I'm going to stick out like a sore thumb. I just brought a cocktail dress."

"Darling, you obviously don't know Trudi." The brunette shook her head. "She would never do anything as crass as hold a costume party."

"And if she did we'd come as something other than ourselves." The blonde turned to her companions. "Do you remember Leila's party? I so enjoyed the can-can costumes. We could go in those again."

"There is no costume party," the redhead reminded her.

"Oh."

Seeing the blonde's face fall in disappointment, Joy almost wished there was a costume party. "Maybe next time," she offered softly.

The older woman's smile was as bright as her banana colored hair.

"Ladies, I'm sorry. I still don't understand what I can do for you."

The blonde and brunette looked as if they were about to say something, but the redhead held up a hand, silencing them. "I've told you two over and over again, let me handle these initial meetings. All you do with your chatter is confuse our goddaughters."

"Goddaughter?" Joy's smile drooped a bit, and a faint headache began to stir behind her eyes.

The redhead nodded encouragingly. "Joy, you see, we're here to help you."

"Help me raise money for Ripples?" Joy asked hopefully.

"Oh, no. We're here to help you find your own true love," the redhead said as the other two bobbed their heads in agreement. "We're your fairy godmothers."

Joy tried to laugh. This was a joke. Max must be behind it Despite his being a psychiatrist, he had always enjoyed tormenting her, trying to convince her that she needed his psychiatric help. "Okay, you three. The joke's over. Tell my dear brother it didn't work."

"Dear, we're not joking." The redhead did indeed look deadly serious. "We've been watching you for quite sometime."

Obviously not able to remain silent, the brunette piped in, "And we know—"

The blonde cut her off. "Yes, we know that you're not happy. You're missing something."

Like a tennis match, the two took off, bouncing one's sentence after the other's.

"You're missing a good man."

"Not that we're saying you need a man to make you complete."

"Certainly not. This is the new millennium, and women have learned to stand on their own two feet."

"And you've done a great job."

"But you need —"

"Yes, you need something more—"

"*Someone* more."

"And we're—"

"Girls." The redhead had obviously had enough. The two shut up.

Joy was grateful. Trying to watch the two of them as they talked had been like trying to watch a high speed tennis ball lob back and forth on the court. Her headache was going to be complicated by a stiff neck.

"Now," said the redhead, once again in charge of the very odd, probably crazy, trio. Maybe they were three of Max's patients, escapees from some asylum. Did they even have asylums anymore?

"Joy." The redhead pulled her from her ruminations. "We realize that this is all confusing, but we know you've read Grace's books, so we know you know how this works. In case you hadn't guessed, I'm Myrtle, she," Myrtle gestured to the blonde, "is Blossom and this is Fern." The brunette nodded.

"We've been looking for your Mr. Right for quite sometime, and we've finally found him. The problem was he didn't really look like a *right*—"

"More like a wrong. There were quite a few strikes against him."

"But there was the wish to consider."

"And you would be an answer to one, despite the strikes against the other."

"Helen, for instance," Blossom muttered.

"Plus he was badly burned by—"

"Girls," Myrtle said, and the sisters fell silent as Myrtle continued. "Suffice to say, that despite some hurdles that will have be to overcome, we have found the perfect man for you. And despite the problems you might have to face, you know we'll be right beside you every step of the way."

It was too much. Joy didn't know if she should take some aspirin—or maybe a valium—or call Max for a reference. Maybe she should call Grace, since the trio claimed to be her brainchildren. The tempo of her headache picked up speed as she considered what she should do next. Were the three women the crazy ones, or was she? "I don't understand what precisely is going on, but I wish you'd all leave. I have an important party—"

"Full of important people with deep pockets," Blossom said, nodding as if she knew what was going on.

"I can't deal with this joke. Tell Max I said, *Ha, Ha.*"

"Sweetheart, we'll let you get ready for your party, but we'll be back to talk to you soon." The redhead, Myrtle, smiled. "We just wanted to drop in and say hello before the fun begins."

The three disappeared in the blink of an eye. They were either very quiet and *very* quick, or they were really fairy—

Joy shut off the thought. She would be crazy if she believed they were really fairy godmothers. And crazy is just what Max, and his sick sense of humor, wanted her to think she was, so she wouldn't give him the satisfaction. She was going to take some aspirin, get dressed and go to this party, where she would reach into all those lovely, deep pockets, taking as much money as possible for Ripples. And, most of all, she was going to forget this odd scene had ever been played out.

That's exactly what she was going to do.

***

Half an hour later, she strode down the hall, dressed, headache numbed by aspirin, and her mind on the party, *not* on the fairies. She wasn't going to think about them, she told herself over and over as she did just that. A physical jolt pulled her from her sanity impairment worries.

"Darn!" she swore.

It was the only word Joy could manage as she began the long descent to the ground. The noise was loud; clattering plates were accompanied by the tinkling of silverware and the shattering of glasses.

Joy landed on her well-padded rump. Momentarily stunned, she sat surrounded by the remains of what must have been the dinner's appetizers. She'd done it again. Actually, she hadn't done it this time. It was a combination of fairy befuddlement, and the small form in a blue jumper huddled against the wall.

"Are you okay?" Joy simultaneously asked the woman who had been carrying the tray, and the little girl who had instigated the three-way collision.

Two red braids bobbed with the rhythm of the nodding head, but no words escaped her.

"I'm just fine," said the woman. "But if her," she jerked her hand toward the girl, "mother finds out what just happened there will be—"

"It was an accident," Joy told the woman firmly. "Everyone has accidents. Since all three of us are okay, I guess our only casualty is a few plates and glasses." Joy smiled at the little girl, but there was no answering expression. The child stood motionless, soundlessly surveying the damage.

From her inelegant seat on the floor, Joy was in the perfect position to pick up the pieces, and she did so, talking to the little girl, ignoring the fact the child hadn't said a word to her or had moved an inch from her spot on the wall.

"Now, you might think that this bumping was a fluke..." Joy waited for the lady to supply her name.

"Martha," the woman finally said.

"Martha. If that's what you think, why then you have another think coming. I'm here to tell you that if it hadn't been the two of you, it would have been something else. I seem to have the ability to fall over nothing."

Though she was talking to Martha, Joy kept her eye on the little girl. "Why, just the other day I was licking an envelope, sending a letter to my brother, and the paper cut my tongue. Can you imagine? A paper cut on your tongue? Hurt like the dickens. Now it takes an especially klutzy person to paper cut their tongue - the type of person who goes tripping over little girls who are only doing what little girls are supposed to do."

Martha gave a reluctant snort, and what might have been the beginning of a smile flitted across her face.

Joy glanced over her shoulder, but the child still had an air of terror in her eyes. "Why, Martha, didn't you know that everything in the world has a purpose? Children are here to run and scream and laugh and make messes. Older brothers are here to torment sisters."

Thinking of her older brothers reminded her of Max and brought the three supposed fairies to mind. For a split second Joy thought she saw them standing just behind the little girl, but in the next blink of her eyes she was once again alone with Martha and the silent child.

Now she was seeing things. It was all Max's fault. She had no idea how he'd bribed three strange women into playing along with his joke, but he was going to pay—and pay big. "But any self-respecting sister knows how to outsmart brothers."

She looked up again at the little girl. "Do you have any brothers or sisters?"

Braids swaying, the little girl shook her head.

"Do you have a name?"

A shy nod this time. "Sophie. Mother hates the way that sounds. She's the only one who calls me Sophia, but really I'm just plain old Sophie." The words were soft, hesitant, but it was a start.

Joy scratched her chin and looked at the child with mock consideration. "I think you're right. You're definitely a Sophie. Why a Sophia would be a quiet mouse of a girl who didn't do anything but sit in a corner all day. I can tell you're the kind of girl who likes to run and shout. Why I even believe you might be the kind of girl who likes to go fishing." Despite her own problems—pseudo-fairies and practical joking brothers—Joy couldn't resist trying to ease a smile onto the child's face.

Needing to save the world was one of her many problems that Max was forever hounding her about. But Joy didn't think it truly qualified as a problem. She didn't like to see people who were hurting or unhappy, neither did Max. He tried to heal the world with psychiatry; by poking around in their brains. Joy preferred working at making people's lives better, so maybe they'd learn to find their happiness on their own.

Sophie shook her head. "I've never fished. Mama thinks I should be a Sophia."

Joy dramatically looked the girl over. "Well, I've studied these things for many years, and I can tell you that you most certainly aren't the kind of girl to stay in a corner for too long. What does your Daddy say?"

"He doesn't say anything."

Joy's heart broke, more for what she heard behind the words than because of the words themselves. "Well, I do, and I know. I was the kind of girl who was always getting in trouble. I can tell a kindred spirit when I see one."

"What's a kindred spirit?" Sophie took a step towards Joy.

"Someone who knows how you feel."

Sophie looked thoughtful. "Then you're my kindred spirit, too."

"I thought so." Joy and Martha had finished putting the evidence of the disaster on the tray. "Now, I have to take this back and see if I can help Martha find something else to serve. But maybe you could meet me in the kitchen tomorrow after breakfast and we can see about teaching you how to fish."

"Do you mean it?" Sophie asked, doubt in her eyes.

"My dear, kindred spirit, you should know right now, I never say anything I don't mean." She struggled from her knees to her feet, tray in hand, ignoring Martha's attempts to take it. "Now, I'll see you tomorrow in the kitchen half an hour after breakfast. And don't wear a frilly dress. Jeans and a t-shirt are what you're going to need."

A smile burst out on the little girl's face. "I'll see you in the morning."

Joy started back into the kitchen, warmed by the little girl's smile. Martha gave her a strange look, but didn't try to take the tray again.

"Are you really going fishing with the girl?"

"It appears that I am."

That hint of a smile once again playing across her face, Martha said, "Well, I guess I could be persuaded to pack a lunch."

"Peanut butter and jelly?"

Martha gave her another odd look. "Just who are you? You're not anything like Mrs. St. John's normal guests."

"Martha, you've learned the truth so quickly. I'm not anyone's normal anything." Joy laughed and Martha joined in, her face covered in a broad smile, not just a hint of one.

"So what are we going to do about an appetizer?" Joy asked, purposely using we, not you. Mrs. St. John strikes me as the type that will expect everything just so, no excuses."

"Then it's lucky for us this disaster struck before we served the entree. Instead of salad, I'll thaw some consume in the microwave and serve that. Her high and mightiness will never know the difference."

"What do you know about the little girl?" Joy asked. She brushed the remains of the salad, broken shards and all, into the trash.

"Now, there's a sad story. The little girl is a casualty of greed. The misses and her ex fought long and hard over custody of poor Miss Sophia. The misses won and the little girl moved here last year. She's a quiet one, forever lurking about the shadows, which is just how Ms. St. John likes it.

"As a matter of fact, today's accident was the first bit of fluster the child has caused in the entire year she's been here. She mainly stays in her rooms with her nanny." As she spoke, Martha bustled about the kitchen, a flurry of motion.

"You can't blame this accident on Sophie." No, Joy was going to blame Max, Grace, and Grace's fairies. "I was lost in thought and hurrying down the hall— a deadly combination. To be honest, accidents seem to find me all on their own." Joy had long ago come to accept that particular foible about herself.

The way she looked at it, there were things that could change and then there were things a person was just stuck with. In her case, accidents were one of the latter.

Thinking of the accident reminded her of fishing. She was going to have to sneak out and buy some poles. She'd seen a great pond about a mile from the St. John home, so a fishing hole was no problem.

Martha began to refill the tray. "Ms. St. John is probably wondering where you are."

"Rats," Joy cried, already racing from the kitchen. "Sorry

again Martha."

She hurried down the hall. She wasn't looking forward to this meal, but it went with the job. Catching her breath outside the formal dining room doors, Joy smoothed her hair and took a deep breath.

Think of the job, not fairies or unhappy little girls, she warned herself. The three fairy impostors were probably waiting for her in the dining room, ready to confess that, prompted by Max, they'd played a prank on her. Well, the last laugh was on them because Joy planned to guilt them out of a whole bunch of money.

She entered the dining room, determined no more disasters would come her way this day. She'd be charming, she'd be sweet, she would not be clumsy. Charming and sweet meant money, and Ripples needed the money.

***

The party had gone well, but that hadn't stopped Joy from spending the night tossing and turning. She sipped her coffee, praying that some reasonable explanation of yesterday's fairy visit would present itself. There had been no short, bright haired women at the party. When she'd asked Trudi, the woman had just given her an odd look, and replied she didn't know anyone who fit the description.

To make matters worse, when she'd climbed wearily back to her room, determined to drive to a twenty-four hour store to buy poles, there had been two fishing poles at the end of her bed. *Martha.* That was the only explanation, or at least, it was the only explanation Joy wanted to accept. But when she'd asked the cook at breakfast, the answer had been no.

It couldn't be fairies. There was no such thing. Only someone certifiably insane would believe in fairy godmothers.

Joy didn't feel insane. As a matter of fact, she was the most practical person in her family. No, she wasn't insane. But for the life of her, she couldn't decide how Max could have orchestrated the fairy prank, or why he would have, for that matter. No, she—

Joy's worries took a backseat as she sensed, more than heard, someone else enter the room. Without turning she said, "Good morning, Sophie. I hope you remembered to dress for the fish. They don't like to be caught by anyone too fancy."

She turned. Sophie stood against the wall, a tentative smile on her face. Her hair was in neat little braids, a crisp pair of jeans and a designer polo shirt. "Mother threw away all my t-shirts," she said. "Is this okay?"

Joy could see the fear of rejection in those beautiful little blue eyes. She gave Sophie her best reassuring smile. "You look just right. Not too messy, not too fancy. The fish will love you. She stood. "Are you ready?"

Sophie nodded.

"Well, then, let's get this show on the road."

Two blue gill later, they sat flicking their poles in the water. "Won't Mother be mad if she finds you're out here?"

Joy laughed. "I doubt she'll notice as long as I'm back in time for lunch."

"But if she did, she might not give you your money," Sophie continued stubbornly.

"Maybe. But I've gotten money out of tighter pockets than hers, so don't worry." Joy laughed. Being a first rate klutz and money machine wouldn't have seemed to go hand in hand, but Joy had found a way to combine her talents, much to her family's dismay. With Max being a psychiatrist, and her brother Nick a lawyer, Joy didn't think she'd ever find a comfortable spot for herself. Eventually she'd found her niche, maybe not as prestigious as her brothers, but it was hers and she liked it.

"Really, it's nothing to worry about," Joy said with a smile.

Despite her obvious worry, Sophie smiled back. "Let's go back anyway."

"Okay, you slave driver, you win." They reeled in their lines, and the fish were placed in a little bucket. They walked back towards the house with a slow, lazy gait.

"I miss my daddy," Sophie said out of the blue.

"I'm sure he misses you too."

Sophie nodded. "Mother wouldn't."

"I'm sure you're mother loves you." How could anyone not love this sweet little girl?

Sophie brows together, unsure. "Maybe."

Joy dropped the poles and knelt down. "Listen to me, your mother might not be the most motherly mom I've ever seen, but sometimes that happens. That doesn't mean she doesn't love you.

"It sounds like your dad loves you lots, too, and I'm sure you'll be with him again. And you have me, a kindred spirit, someone to understand and hug you."

So saying, Joy swept the child into her embrace. For once her ample padding stood her in good stead. It cushioned the fragile spirit she hugged tight. "You and I are going to be great friends."

"But you won't stay. When Mother's given you the money today, you'll leave."

"The thing with kindred spirits is they never are far apart." She hugged the girl again. They made their way back up to the house.

For a moment, Joy almost wished the three women from yesterday were really fairy godmothers. If they were real, she'd wish that Sophie would have a family and feel loved, really loved.

"Done," a voice seemed to whisper in her head. Joy turned around, expecting to see someone walking behind her and Sophie, but all she saw was Trudi St. John's well manicured lawn, framed by woods in the background.

A small shiver climbed her spine, but Joy pushed it aside. She was not going to allow Max's weird sense of humor to spook her.

***

Joy sat in a chaise lounge pool-side, across from her hostess. Her bags were packed, and she was ready to hit the road.

The party had been a huge success. The funds she'd raised by rubbing shoulders with Trudi St. John's friends would keep Ripples running for a few more months anyway. Though she'd kept Ripples in the black, Joy didn't feel a sense of accomplishment. She was leaving with money, but she was leaving behind the saddest set of brown eyes she'd ever seen.

Last night she'd learned that Trudi St. John's eyes were as hard as her daughter's were sad. Joy forced herself to smile as she said, "Thank you again for hosting the event. Ripples will be able to do a lot with the money your guests contributed."

"I haven't had a chance to talk to you about my donation." Trudi leaned forward.

Joy felt distinctly uneasy. Trudi was making her feel hunted. "You've already done so much, but Ripples, and all the people it helps, will be happy to let you do more."

"Yes, I have a small request to make of you, before I write my check. You see, I need someone to take Sophie to her father's. William proposed last night." She flashed a huge diamond ring.

Joy didn't need to be an expert in gems to realize how expensive the ring was. But expense didn't necessarily equal passion. She remembered William from last night. The term cold fish came to mind.

"He's adamant that we marry as soon as possible. His business takes him all over the world, and he wants me at his side. Marcie, the child's nanny, refuses to make the trip to take her to her father, and I don't have time. William wants to leave as soon as possible. And it's not as if I can take a child with me."

"Are you asking me if I would consider taking Sophie to her father?" *Good heavens! What kind of woman would entrust her child to a virtual stranger*?

Trudi, who was sprawled in the chaise lounge, lowered her sun glasses and peered at Joy over their rims. "I wasn't exactly asking; I was bargaining. I know Ripples needs my support—"

"And in order to gain that support you think I'll take a child I hardly know to a man I've never met?"

"I think you're a woman who understands back scratching," Trudi said, slipping her glasses back over her eyes.

"You aren't hesitant about letting you're little girl travel with a stranger?" Joy knew if she had a girl as precious as Sophie she would never, never let her go with just anyone.

"Hardly that. I've known Nick for years, and I think I've even met Max once or twice." Trudi tapped her beautifully manicured nails on the arm of the chair. "And I've followed your work through them, and through some other acquaintances. That's why I decided to host this fundraiser. And of course we've gotten to know each other while we worked on this project. You're a better choice than just sticking Sophia on a plane, and letting her make the trip on her own."

"I just don't know," Joy hedged, though she knew she was going to say yes. If she said no, who would Trudi palm Sophie off on then?

"Then you won't do it?" Obviously unused to being denied, shock registered on Trudi's face.

Joy crossed her fingers behind her back, hoping she was playing this hand right. "I'd be happy to take Sophie to her father. This is a permanent move, isn't it?"

Trudi nodded. "William's business takes him all over the world, so naturally I'll travel with him. It would be impossible to take a child with me."

Joy held her smile inside, gripping it with the fiercest control she'd ever exercised. "Well, can you have the papers ready by the time we leave?"

"Papers?" Trudi looked confused.

"Of course. If Mr. St. John is taking over permanent care of Sophie, he'll need all the legal forms dotted and signed. What if something happened to her and you couldn't be reached, traveling like you're planning? He needs to be the custodial parent on paper."

"I'll call my lawyer and have him draw them up. I'm sure he can fax over the proper documents."

"He'd take care of it that fast?"

Trudi laughed. "Honey, remember the old saying money talks? Well, it doesn't just talk, it shouts."

Joy almost wished the fairy godmothers were real so she could thank them. Sophie was going back to the father. The child spoke with affection about him, and Joy couldn't imagine he could be a worse parent than Trudi.

Her little kindred spirit was going to be removed from this stifling, oppressive atmosphere. Joy wanted to laugh and dance for the sheer happiness that welled within her heart.

"I'll have Ripples' check ready along with Sophie and her things," Trudi added, coming to the end of her monologue about William and all the things they were going to do.

"That would be wonderful."

"I'll have directions to Gabriel's, and money to cover your expenses for the trip," Trudi added.

"That would be fine. Have you told Sophie yet?"

"Oh, why don't you see if you can track her down? Tell her I'll be up later to say goodbye."

Joy left then, turning her back to conceal the smile she just couldn't hold in any longer. Anger warred with her sense of accomplishment. Sophie was a treasure that Trudi had never recognized. Joy only prayed that Gabriel St. John would.

Still smiling, she ran down the hall of the cold mansion, looking for Sophie.

"Joy."

She knew before she turned around that they were back. She turned, but instead of the three fake-fairy ladies, only one stood in the quiet hall.

"Myrtle?"

"I'm glad you found the poles this morning. That trip was just what Sophie needed. We were worried about how to get her back to her father without upsetting her, but she likes you. She'll go with no fuss."

"You set this up?"

"Of course we did. You made a wish, remember?"

"But—"

"Joy, I know you're still trying to think of a rational explanation - rational seems to be something you Aaronson's excel at. You've tried everything from blaming Max to thinking you're nuts. Of course, Grace had a hard time at first as well, and she created us, so we'll excuse your disbelief for now."

"You're *not* real," Joy said. No one in the twenty-first century had fairy godmothers...myths, fairy tales, that's all they were. "*You're not real*," she repeated, though she wasn't sure who she was trying to convince, Myrtle, or herself.

"As real as you are, in our own way. I left my sisters behind because sometimes they can be a little much."

Joy couldn't help the smile that tugged at her lips.

Myrtle's smile echoed hers. "Okay, we can all be a bit much. It's Grace's fault, really. We were created in her imagination. Now, about what we're going to do next. I think it would be easier if we could just get past all the mental doubts, and thoughts of brotherly jokes and mental instability. Call Max and Grace."

"Call them?"

"Before you leave with Sophie, call them. Ask them how they got together."

"I don't have to ask. Grace had problems with some characters and went to Max for his psychiatric opinion and..." Joy stopped. "You three were the problem?"

"Grace seemed to worry that she was sanity impaired when we showed up. Just call them and we can get past that nonsense." Myrtle disappeared as quickly and quietly as yesterday.

Call Grace and Max? How would she start?

Max, I'm seeing fairies...

ABOUT THE AUTHOR

Holly Fuhrmann lives in Erie, PA and is the mother of four children, which makes her a leading authority on sanity-challenged writers. She is the author of six books. If you enjoyed *Mad About Max*, please be sure to watch for *Magic for Joy* in November, 2000.

Holly loves to hear from her readers. You can visit her home page on the web at: http://members.aol.com/hfur/index.html, or you may write her at: PO Box 11102, Erie, PA 16514-1102.